Tris & Izzie

Mette Ivie Harrison

EGMONT
USA
NEW YORK

EGMONT
We bring stories to life

First published by Egmont USA, 2011
443 Park Avenue South, Suite 806
New York, NY 10016

Copyright © Mette Ivie Harrison, 2011
All rights reserved

1 3 5 7 9 8 6 4 2

www.egmontusa.com
www.metteivieharrison.com

Library of Congress Cataloging-in-Publication Data

Harrison, Mette Ivie, 1970-
Tris and Izzie / Mette Ivie Harrison.
p. cm.
Summary: When sixteen-year-old Izzie makes a love potion for her best
friend, she is unaware that she, like her long-dead father, has real magic, and
while she is trying to sort out her friends' love lives she must also deal with
monsters that have her magical scent and want to destroy her.
ISBN 978-1-60684-173-0 (hardcover)
ISBN 978-1-60684-257-7 (electronic book)
[1. Magic—Fiction. 2. Interpersonal relations—Fiction. 3. High schools—
Fiction. 4. Schools—Fiction. 5. Monsters—Fiction.] I. Title.
PZ7.H25612Tri 2011
[Fic]—dc22
2010051588

Printed in the United States of America
CPSIA tracking label information:
Printed in August 2011 at Berryville Graphics, Berryville, Virginia

To Scott Abbott

Chapter 1

Mark caught me in a big hug from behind as I closed my locker. "Guess who?" he said.

"Um, my fabulous captain-of-the-Tintagel-High-basketball-team boyfriend with the darkest, deepest eyes ever?" I said.

He turned me around so I could look into those very eyes. "Got it in one," he said. He kissed me lightly on the nose and let me go.

"Hey, there's a reason I get straight A's," I teased. Mark had trouble keeping his GPA high enough to stay on the team, but I tutored him when I could. Too bad we didn't have any classes together this year.

"You are smart and pretty," said Mark. "What a lucky guy I am."

I'm just over five feet tall, dark-haired, and dark-eyed. My dad picked out my name, Isolde, which means "fair lady," before I was born. He used to tease me that it was just like me to be contrary, even then.

I miss my dad a lot these days. You'd think it would get easier, after ten years, but it doesn't. Sometimes when I am with Mark, it hurts the most, because I think of how much Dad would have wanted to tease me about him.

"You're practically perfect, in fact," Mark went on. "Seems a little unfair, don't you think, Branna?"

I hadn't seen Branna until then. She is almost six feet tall and has huge shoulders from swimming butterfly, but Mark is even taller and broader across the shoulders than she is. He can block her out completely, or anyone else, really, which is why he is such a great basketball player. He just holds his hands up and no one can get around him to the basket.

"Yeah, totally unfair. If Izzie weren't so nice, everyone would hate her," said Branna. She gave a twisted smile, and I could tell that something was wrong, because she's my best friend. She moved off with her arms wrapped around her middle, and she barely looked at me.

Usually, we were the Three Musketeers. Mark and I had been dating for over a year, but Branna always hung out with us. Branna and I had been superglue close since kindergarten, when I moved to Tintagel in midyear and started getting picked on because I was so small. Branna had protected me then, and I wished I could return the favor now. If only she would tell me what was bothering her.

I saw that Branna was headed toward her locker, which was up on the second floor.

"Uh, Mark, love you." I blew him a quick kiss. "Gotta go." I started running up the stairs behind Branna.

I turned once to see Mark watching me appreciatively. "Love it when you run, Izzie!" he said.

I blushed, but really, what is wrong with your boyfriend noticing that you look good? I don't know why it made me uncomfortable. It wasn't as if Mark was one of those guys who thought of his girlfriend as just a body.

I caught up with Branna by the second-floor bathrooms.

"What's up?" I asked, reaching for her arm.

She pulled away from me, and there was a moment when I remembered how much bigger than me Branna is.

"Branna, please tell me. I can help, I swear!" There had been something wrong for months, and the most I could get out of Branna was that it wasn't my fault. She said it had to do with someone else, but she wouldn't tell me who. In ten years of us being best friends, there had never been something between us that we couldn't talk about.

She turned around and loomed over me. "What makes you think you can do anything for me, Izzie? What are you, the queen of the world?"

"Maybe," I said, looking up at her. "I'm the queen of the high school, at least, since I'm dating Mark, and he's the king." I'm not afraid of her. No matter how big she is, I know she won't hurt a fly. That's just the way Branna is.

"Fine." She closed her eyes, and when she opened them again, it was like she'd put on a mask so she wouldn't hurt anymore. "There is something."

"Really?" I clapped my hands like a little kid. I wanted so badly to do something for Branna in return for all the times she had been there for me. "Anything. Tell me."

Branna looked up and down the hallway, then nodded for

me to follow her. We ended up tucked into the alcove by the janitor's closet.

"So?" I said.

"It's Mel Melot," Branna said, making a face.

Mel is short and has spiky blond hair and a goatee. He joined Mark's posse this year, but I'm not sure why Mark let him. Mel annoyed me with his stupid, sly jokes. Mark told me that if I really disliked him, he would "exile" him, which meant that no one would speak a word to him without Mark's permission. I was still thinking about it.

"What about him?" I asked.

"I think he's using magic," said Branna.

"What? That's impossible." Branna knew my mom was a witch, but she was the only one who did. I didn't even tell her until sixth grade, after we had known each other for years and years.

"Well, I hope so," said Branna.

"I didn't think there was anyone else who even believed in it," I said, "let alone had it."

"Yeah, me either," said Branna.

When I was five, Mom and I moved away from the magical place where she and Dad had gotten married and where I had lived my whole life. I don't really remember it much because I was so little. Mom said it was too painful to stay where all the memories were. Dad died just after I failed the test for magic that was supposed to help figure out what kind I had. I guess magic can skip a generation or even fade out completely. No one knows the reason, but it's why there's less magic in the world now than there used to be. It's hard to live without magic surrounded by magic people, Mom says.

I believe her, but it's also hard to live knowing magic is real surrounded by other people who don't know about it and have never seen it, except for the effects of Mom's secret potions. They all think it's just because the hospital here is so great, but we didn't win national awards until Mom started driving ambulances. The doctors don't even realize how much she has to do with their success.

Ever since I can remember, Mom has drilled into me the danger of talking about magic openly. If we did, she says, the cameras would descend, and we wouldn't have a private life anymore. Crackpots would want her to help them with their potions. I would be laughed at and, if people thought she was crazy enough, maybe even taken away from her.

"What kind of magic?" I asked Branna, trying to control my panic. "Did you see him use it?"

"No," said Branna.

I could tell that Branna was still avoiding telling me the whole truth about what was bothering her, but this was important, and it had to be dealt with now. "Tell me what happened."

A couple of people passed us, headed to class. Branna waited until they were gone. "I was talking to a girl from the swim team," she said. "She said that Mel told her he had magic."

"And she believed him?"

"He claimed he had a bottle of wine that you could drink from and it would never go empty," said Branna. "Is that possible?"

Even though Mom was a witch, I didn't know about all the kinds of magic there were. I knew she could use potions that she made herself if the ingredients were natural things and she followed the right recipe, but she couldn't make objects come to life or wishes come true. She couldn't change the past or control the future. And she had no power over the elements—air, fire, water, and earth.

I knew that there were different kinds of magic only because of the fairy tales that Mom used to read me when I was little. She would shake her head about one story that had gotten it wrong and nod gently at another that clearly had it right. When I asked her directly, Mom tended to clam up and mutter something about my not needing to know that.

Since we moved here, I had never seen anyone use magic. A part of me was horrified at the thought of someone openly using magic here, but another part of me was just plain curious.

"She said she went over to his house and he got the bottle out," Branna added before I could answer her. "They apparently drank from it all night, and it was still full in the morning when she stumbled out, hungover."

"He could easily have tricked her," I said. "He could have had a bunch of bottles that all looked the same and just switched them out." It was easier to use tricks than real magic, which was why Hollywood was still making movies the way it did. There were witches in Hollywood, Mom said, but they were more into youth potions than special effects.

"He could have," said Branna. But she didn't look convinced.

I wasn't convinced, either. If Mel didn't have magic and was just saying he did, that was one thing. But if he did have magic and he was going around telling everyone, that was something else.

"We need to be sure," I said. This wasn't something I could tell Mark about. He didn't know about Mom being a witch. He didn't know anything about magic being real, and I wanted it to stay that way. It wasn't like I had magic myself, so I wasn't keeping any important truths from him, even if Branna thought I was.

"I saw him this morning, before you got here." Branna drove her own car to school these days, instead of taking the bus.

"Where is he?" I asked.

"Over in the deadhead halls. With another freshman."

"You don't think he would bring a magic bottle of wine to school, do you?" That would be extremely stupid and supremely arrogant. Unfortunately, that was in keeping with what I knew of Mel so far.

The bell was about to ring, but I started running toward the other wing of the school. Branna followed me. We were both going to be late for class. But what else could I do? Mom would want me to do this. Keeping magic secret was important.

Chapter 2

We ran past the office and the auditorium, and then turned left at the second hall where the deadheads hung out by the bathrooms. When we got closer, I stopped and put out a hand for Branna to stay behind me. If Mel had a magic bottle of wine, who knew what else he might have? A magic knife? Or sword?

Branna had no defense against him except herself, but I had a special protection potion I carried in my backpack. Mom had insisted I start carrying it to school when we moved here, after Dad died. That was when she got her job as an ambulance driver and started using her potions to save people's lives.

I think Mom still feels guilty about what happened with Dad. She thought we both just had the flu. But then he died, and she had to make up a potion to save me. It almost wasn't enough at that point, because I was sick for weeks.

After that, she became paranoid about keeping me safe, so now she sends me to school with the potion. I don't know exactly what it's supposed to do, but Mom assured me that if I was ever threatened, all I had to do was pop the cork and throw it at whoever was trying to hurt me.

I could hear Mel's voice down the hall now. I moved as quietly as possible, so as not to surprise him and have him turn his magic—if he had magic—on us.

"We have lots of interesting things at home," said Mel. "My parents came from Alsace-Lorraine and they brought some of the last, best magic of the old country."

A girl giggled. I could smell the cloying, overly sweet odor of whatever Mel had on him. They were shadowy figures still, not clear enough for me to recognize the girl or to see the object Mel was holding in his hand.

"If you come over to my house tonight, I could show you all my magic," said Mel.

I rolled my eyes. What a line.

I put my hand on the vial of potion and pulled it out of my pocket. I had held on to it a few times in the past, when I was walking home in the dark or when I heard weird noises in the house while Mom wasn't home. But I had never actually cracked the cork before.

Mom told me that the potion wouldn't kill anyone—or make them melt, which I asked after I saw *The Wizard of Oz* for the first time. It would just keep me safe from any threat, and I figured that included Mel Melot.

"Izzie," whispered Branna, behind me.

I turned around and put a finger to my lips.

Her eyes were wide and she gestured for me to get out of

the way. She had to outweigh Mel Melot by about a hundred pounds. I'm sure she thought she was the one to handle him.

But I was stubborn enough to shake my head at her. I didn't want her to get in trouble with the principal because she got into a fistfight with Mel. There was a zero-tolerance policy for violence at the school, and she could end up being suspended.

The girl whispered something.

"I like freshman girls," said Mel. "They're just easier to talk to. Not so judgmental."

Not so smart, I thought.

I was definitely going to tell Mark to exile Mel. But for now, I had to stop him. This girl was young and obviously gullible, and Mel was taking advantage of her, magically.

In fact, Mel was violating one of the rules of magic that Mom has told me about over and over again, even though I don't have magic myself. It's a rant left over from when she used to live with lots of magical people. Magic isn't to be used to manipulate or deceive. Magic is a source of good, and it's people like Mel Melot using it wrongly that made other people burn witches in the old days.

That was when people with magic started to withdraw into the pockets around the world where they live now. Mom says that their isolation also helps police the magic, so no single magic user becomes too powerful and takes control of the non-magical world. She got out because she was just a witch, and even so, she had to promise she would use her magic to help people, magical and non-magical alike.

I lifted the vial to my mouth and used my teeth to tear out the cork. There wasn't any flavor that I could detect, which surprised me. When my mom gave me the healing potion after my dad died, I had a smoky, sooty taste in my mouth for days. I also had terrible dreams about a forty-foot-tall serpent with red and gold sparkling scales saying my name.

But eventually, the dreams went away, and I always assumed they were an aftereffect of the potion. I hadn't taken any other potions besides that one. But I had seen Mom make them, and I knew she sometimes put snake scales in them. I figured that might have triggered my dream in some way. If there had been newts in the potion, I would probably have dreamed about giant newts instead.

Branna scuffed her foot against the wall, and Mel jerked upright, craning down the hallway. "Who's there?" he asked. He was reaching for his pocket, and I reacted swiftly.

Hands shaking, heart thundering, I threw the potion in his face and stepped to the side.

But nothing happened.

No screaming.

No frozen human statue.

Had Mom's potion lost its effect after all this time?

I saw Mel's hand slip back into his pocket, along with a cigarette. Not a knife. Not a sword.

Maybe I'd gone a little overboard with the potion. Would Mom be mad at me when I told her I'd wasted it? But why hadn't it done anything? All these years, I thought it would protect me, and it was useless in the end.

For a moment, I doubted my mom's magic. Could it all be pretend—all the potions she made, all her secretiveness? Or maybe Mel hadn't been enough of a direct threat?

"What was that?" asked Mel, wiping at his face. "Did you just spit at me? That's gross."

"Leave him alone!" shouted the freshman girl. "What do you think you're doing?" She put an arm around Mel's chest.

But he shoved her off kind of roughly. "Get out of here," he told her.

She hesitated a moment and then left, giving me a dirty look on her way out.

"Show me that bottle," I said to Mel. Just because he didn't have a weapon didn't mean he wasn't dangerous, magic or no magic.

"I don't have to," said Mel.

Branna came around to my front and gave him a menacing look, just like the one she had used on my tormenters in kindergarten. "Show it to her," she said.

Mel's lips twisted together. "Fine. Look at it," he said, holding out the bottle to me.

It was about the size of a normal wine bottle, the glass tinged green. It did not look particularly magical, but it did look really old. I held the label up to the light, but the words were so faded I couldn't read them. "What's in this?" I asked.

"The good stuff," said Mel. "For the girls, you know."

"Right." I sniffed the bottle. Definitely not wine. It was something stronger.

"Hey, what are you doing?" asked Mel, trying to grab it back from me.

Branna kept him from moving. She stood between him and me, and I'm sure she would have been glad to pin him against the wall if he touched me.

I turned the bottle upside down, but nothing came out.

I squinted and looked inside the bottle. There was definitely something there. I wiggled the bottle back and forth and could hear sloshing.

"It has a special no-drip cap," said Mel.

"There is no cap on this right now," I said. How stupid did he think I was?

"Well, the bottle is designed specially—" he tried again.

I gave him the bottle back. "Drink it," I said.

"I already had plenty," said Mel.

"Drink it," said Branna, looming over him.

"Fine." Mel took a couple of swallows.

"Drink more," I said.

Mel kept drinking. But when he handed it back to me, it had the same amount of liquid in it as before, .

It was definitely magic—no reason to doubt that.

I still didn't know what had made Mom's potion inactive. Maybe she'd have an explanation when I told her about it.

"It's magic. Very valuable. A family heirloom," said Mel, his tone commanding. "It's important to me."

"I guess you shouldn't have brought it to school to get freshman girls drunk, then, should you?" I took the bottle and threw it against the cement blocks that were the walls of the school. It didn't shatter. It just thunked back at me.

Mel took a deep breath, as if relieved.

"Let me try that," said Branna, picking up the bottle.

"Please," said Mel, his attitude changing from belligerent to begging. "Please. I could get you something really nice. A potion or something. I'd make it worth your while. You don't know how much trouble I will be in if you break that."

I shook my head. "I don't need any potions from him," I said to Branna.

She lifted the bottle.

"No!" shouted Mel, and he looked really afraid: trembling, sweating. It made me feel sorry for him, a little.

Branna hesitated. "What kind of potions?" she asked.

"Any kind," said Mel. "Strength potion—or—or—a love potion!"

Branna tensed.

"Yeah, a love potion," Mel went on. "I can make anyone fall in love with you. Anyone at all. I just need a bit of him and a bit of you, and you have to get him to drink something. You want that?"

"Not from you," said Branna. She smashed the bottle against the wall, and while it didn't shatter, it did fall into several large pieces, which slipped to the ground and started to sizzle. Mel tried to pick them up, but they were disappearing.

I turned away from him.

"You're going to regret this!" Mel shouted after us as we walked back down the hall toward our lockers. "You're both going to regret this someday!"

I didn't worry about that much, because once I told Mark to exile Mel, no one at the school would speak to him again. It had happened before. Mel might hang around for a little while, offering his magic to the dregs, but eventually he'd find another school. And that was fine with me, as long as it was far away from this one and no one could connect me and my mom with his talk of magic.

"Thanks for your help, Branna," I said.

"No problem." She wouldn't look me in the eyes, and I had

a sudden feeling I knew why. She'd done the same thing when Mark had been teasing me: turned away, like she couldn't stand it anymore. It had to be because she was in love with someone—someone she couldn't have. In one moment Mel had put his finger on a problem I had been wondering about for months.

Branna had been content for a while to be the third wheel, going on dates with me and Mark and just hanging out. But now every time she saw us together, it hurt to be reminded of what she didn't have. I should have guessed this. Branna was my best friend. Why hadn't I noticed that she got upset around us as a couple? Probably because I paid attention to Mark. And to how I felt about him.

"You know, a love potion isn't the only way to get the guy of your dreams," I said.

"You already have the guy of your dreams," said Branna bitterly. "What do you know about the need for love potions?"

"I could help, you know. And if it's not someone I know, I could tell Mark. He knows almost everyone."

"I don't want help," said Branna. "From you or Mark."

"How about my mom, then? I could get her to make you a love potion, if you want." Actually, I didn't know if I could do that. Mom had never let me use her potions before. She wouldn't even let me near her potions while she was making them. She said that if I got any of my essence on them, it could invalidate them.

"I don't want a love potion," said Branna.

"But you're in love, right? Wouldn't things be so much easier if he loved you back?"

Branna shook her head. "It tempted me for a moment, but

I wouldn't really want him to love me because of a potion," she said. "It has to come from him or it doesn't matter."

"So, your solution is what?"

"I'll just have to wait," said Branna.

"Wait for what? For him to fall in love with you back? What if he doesn't even know that you love him in the first place? You could spend the next two years with him completely oblivious to you, and then we'll graduate and you'll never know what might have happened. Is that what you want, Branna?" As soon as I said the words, I knew I'd gone too far. I wanted so much to help her, but she wouldn't let me, and now I'd hurt her feelings. Some friend I was.

"I'll live with it," said Branna tightly. Then she walked off.

Mark was such a great guy, and I was so happy with him. It was killing me to see Branna like this. If only . . .

Branna said she didn't want him to fall in love with her because of a potion, but how would she know the difference, once it had happened? It was what a friend would do for a friend who was lonely, right? I just had to figure out how to get a love potion that would work.

Chapter 3

When Dad was alive, Mom would tell me stories and fairy tales about "true love" all the time. She stopped doing it after his death, because it hurt her too much. She's never gotten over him. She doesn't date, and it's not just for my sake. There's no one out there who makes her feel the way my dad did. So she has me, and her job, and her potions. She's always telling me her life is plenty full.

The way I remember hearing it when I was little, Mom and Dad met at a train station in the regular world. They were getting onto trains headed in opposite directions. When their eyes met, they knew they were meant for each other. I guess that's the way it is for people who have magic.

Since Dad had already boarded, he had to push three people out of the way, leave his suitcase behind on the train, and squeeze through the closing doors. Meanwhile, Mom threw a magic freezing potion on everyone on her train, then broke the glass in the door with her high-heeled shoes so she could get out and run to him. Love at first sight.

For a long time when I was in elementary school, I told myself that I was never going to fall in love after the pain I saw Mom go through with Dad.

But that was before Mark.

Mark and I bumped into each other—literally—while Branna and I were shopping at the mall early in our sophomore year. I was looking around at some silver vests that I thought might be magic, and Mark was showing off some of his basketball moves to fans.

Then suddenly all his tall, dark, and handsomeness was staring up at me. His brown eyes were so deep I thought I might fall into them.

"Sorry," he said, getting out from under me. "I wasn't looking where I was going."

I guess I hadn't been, either.

"Here, let me help you." He offered me a hand and set me back on my feet. "Are you all right?"

"I'm fine," I said, embarrassed when his hand brushed briefly against my backside. But not too embarrassed. I grinned up at him.

He said, "I'm Mark King."

"I know who you are," I said. "Everyone knows who you are." I had completely forgotten about Branna until then. She was standing to the side, quiet, like she usually is. She was looking at Mark but not gawking at him like I was.

"This is Branna, my best friend," I said, nodding toward her. "And I'm Izzie."

Mark put out his hand.

"Brangane," said Branna, shaking it. "But everyone calls me Branna."

"It's an unusual name," said Mark.

Branna shrugged. She didn't tell the story often, but it came out when anyone heard her full name. "My parents named me after this great-aunt, who's German. She's rich and she's old, and, well, they wanted me to inherit."

"And did you?" asked Mark.

Branna shook her head. "She's a hundred and three and still kicking. I think she likes writing to my parents and telling them about the latest 5K she's run. She wins her age groups and everything."

"Sounds like a tough old bird," said Mark.

"Yeah. Well," said Branna.

She's not so good at talking to boys, see? It's one of the things I wish she would let me help her with, but she won't practice or anything. She says that what comes naturally will either get her the right guy or it won't, but she won't do anything extra. She says it would be fake, and then the love would be fake, and what would be the point of that?

Branna won't even wear makeup or curl her hair. She puts it in braids to keep it out of her face, not to make herself prettier. Once in a blue moon, she will wear a dress. She doesn't understand that sometimes you have to get a guy's attention first, and then afterward you can let it be more natural.

"So, you want to get a yogurt with us or something?" I asked Mark that day. And he did.

Branna came with us and we had a grand time.

We've lived happily ever after for a year. Me and Mark, I mean. I guess not Branna.

Clearly, she needed help with love. I had experience. She might think that love shouldn't be helped along, but I knew better. In my case, it had been enough to bat my eyelashes, take Mark's arm, and eat yogurt slowly while I laughed at his jokes and leaned really close to him.

But for Branna, it was time to go to the source of all truth. The Internet . . .

I found a site called www.lovepotionsandmore.com that had a recipe for a love potion from someone who claimed to be a "real witch." It sounded like the kind of potion I'd seen my mom put together, and I thought it was worth a try. The other reason I thought there might be a chance it was real was that I knew the magic wasn't in the ingredients, and the Web site didn't claim it was, either.

Whenever I peeked in on my mom making potions, I knew that her magic came out of her as she stirred the ingredients together. And the Web site claimed that if you paid the money, the witch would send out magic through the Internet. All I had to do after that was make sure that I "activated" the potion by putting in a hair or fingernail clipping from each party.

I knew I didn't have magic like Mom did, but Mel Melot had bought that magic wine bottle. He wasn't a witch himself or anything. He just knew enough to go looking for magic and pay for it. My mom didn't want other people knowing about her magic, but not all witches had to be that scrupulous, right? Besides, the recipe was guaranteed to work within the week or my money back. So either Branna would be happy with the right guy in time for the homecoming dance or I'd have my ten dollars.

The ingredients were:

2 T cayenne pepper
1-inch cube fresh minced ginger root
1 cup red wine vinegar (not balsamic—the sourer, the better)

The instructions were simple.

Mix with bamboo spoon over a double boiler until just steaming. Then cool gently, without ice. Add one item taken from each of the lovers. Can be hair, saliva, fingernails, dried skin, etc. Stir and strain. Then add to a drink of any kind except milk.

Why not milk? I didn't know. I wasn't going to use anything alcoholic, however, especially on school property. It said any kind of drink, so I had a bottle of Sprite. It was sweet enough to counteract the vinegar and strong enough to disguise other flavors.

I had Branna's comb. I'd taken it from her after school. It was easy, since we sit together on the bus. The day before I made the potion, I distracted her by pointing out the window; then I dug into the little pocket on the side of her backpack and slipped the comb into my front coat pocket.

There was only one hair caught on it, but I figured it would be enough. I didn't know who the other particle would be from yet, but I could worry about that later.

Mom was scheduled to be at the hospital the next morning for at least six hours, so I had time to practice. Once I'd had breakfast, I got to work. I put on the double boiler, and then I stirred in the ingredients with a bamboo spoon. I wondered what Mom would put into a magical love potion.

Most of her potions were for strength or healing, some for happiness or a positive attitude. I think she once even made a potion to make someone sick, but I wasn't supposed to know about that. Mom muttered something about him confessing an evil plan to her while in the ambulance, and she wanted to make sure he couldn't go through with it. But that's not the way it usually works.

I thought about it, and then remembered Mom didn't call it a love potion at all. She said it was a love "philtre," a French word for an originally French recipe. A few years ago she made one to give as a wedding gift to the daughter of one of the doctors at the hospital. After it was finished, as it was cooling on the stove, she said she was conflicted about it.

"Is it because you're afraid they'll find out you were the one who sent it?" I asked. "That you have real magic?"

Mom said no. She thought they would think it was quaint, but not real.

"Is it because you aren't sure it will work?"

"It will work," Mom said.

"Then why? Is it too expensive?"

"The ingredients aren't expensive in themselves," said Mom.

"Then does it take a lot of magic?"

Mom didn't answer for a while. Then she said, "It has to do with choice, Izzie. I wouldn't want to give magic that would take away someone's choice."

"What about little kids in the ambulance? They can't choose whether to take one of your healing potions or not. Nor can people who are unconscious." I was proud of myself for figuring out a loophole to Mom's argument.

"They want to live. The human body always wants to live," said Mom. "Except—"

"What?" I asked.

"Well, there have been two times when I didn't give a potion that I could have given. Because I was asked not to."

"I thought you said everyone wants to live."

"I said the body wants to live. But there are times when the mind is ready to move on. When people are old enough to make that choice, Izzie, when they have lived a long life and they are choosing death not out of fear or despair but simply out of peace, then I would not force a potion, even on a dying body," said Mom.

"Oh. But these two want to get married. Don't they?" We were looking at a photograph of the smiling bride and groom. Mom had been holding it the whole time, as if memorizing the two faces.

"They want to get married. But do they want to be in love forever?" Mom asked. "That's the question."

"Of course they do," I said. I might have been naive, but I figured anyone who wanted to get married wanted to be in love forever. "Did you and Dad take a love philtre?" I asked.

Mom hesitated for a long moment, then said, "Yes, we did.

But it was after we had been married for a while. Kind of a renewal of vows thing, when you were born."

"Then it must be the best thing to do. Because you and Dad were perfect for each other."

I smiled, but Mom looked away.

She told me while she cleaned up the kitchen that in the old days, when they still had arranged marriages, the mother of the bride would go to a local witch and ask for a love philtre and give it to her daughter and the groom the night before the wedding. It was considered the best wedding gift, because it made sure the bride and groom would be happy with each other, even if they had never met before or even if they hated each other and the only reason they were getting married was that their families wanted them to.

"But to be in love with someone forever, even if they are gone, Izzie—that's a burden. Not everyone can bear it," Mom said finally.

"You think one of them is going to die?" I asked, pointing to the photo.

"I don't think that." Mom sighed. "I just don't know the two of them very well. And the philtre takes away any chance to fall out of love. It's not always a good thing. Sometimes people think they are in love with a person, but he or she turns out to have been hiding something important. Or things change, and it might be easier not to be in love forever."

Mom didn't end up sending the love philtre after all. She decided it was too dangerous, and she couldn't be sure it was the right thing.

I never heard what happened to the couple. I guess you can be perfectly happily married without a love philtre. After all, I hadn't needed one with Mark, and we were fine. But Branna clearly needed something to help her along, and maybe a love potion would be just the thing. With none of the dangers of my mom's real magic.

The timer rang, and I started. The love potion did not look good. It smelled even worse. Had I done something wrong?

I could see the powdered cayenne and the little bits of ginger root floating in it like snow in a ghoulish snow globe. No wonder you were supposed to strain it.

I looked around the kitchen. I didn't think the colander would work, but I finally found some cheesecloth, which I don't think Mom has ever used for making cheese. I got out a glass jar and put the cheesecloth over the top of it, securing the cloth with a rubber band. Then I poured in just a tablespoon of liquid to see what would happen.

The cheesecloth worked great. The liquid in the glass jar looked clear and red, like good wine. Maybe this would work!

I poured in the rest of the potion, then took off the cheesecloth and swished it around.

Then I unwrapped the one hair from Branna's comb and stirred it in.

And—nothing. No sizzle. No flash of lightning to show power.

Suddenly, I was discouraged. What had I been thinking? A love potion off the Internet? By someone who promised she'd put magic in it if I paid her? There was no way this would work. This wasn't a magic wine bottle that would work for anyone. This had to work for two particular people.

I dumped the potion into the sink and sat, morosely

thinking. Then I had an idea. My love potion had been a bust, but that didn't mean a real love philtre wouldn't work.

As far as I knew, Mom still had the love philtre she had almost sent to the bride and groom. I still had a few hours before Mom got home. All I had to do was find the key to the dark maple cabinet in her office, where she kept her potions.

I searched her whole room, looking through her makeup drawer, which was a mess, and her drawer of old lotions. She still had a few of Dad's things tucked away: his hairbrush, which still smelled like him, and his toothbrush and cinnamon toothpaste.

I finally found the key in her underwear drawer. That seemed like a dumb place to hide it, but then again, it was the last place I had thought to look, so it must not be too bad.

I checked my watch and realized I had spent hours looking for the key. Now Mom was supposed to be home in fifteen minutes. But if I worked fast, it might still be okay.

I hurried downstairs and opened the potion cabinet. When I looked inside, I saw that Mom didn't label her bottles. She didn't have to, since she had made them all herself and knew which was which.

I closed my eyes and tried to remember the color of the bottle Mom had poured the love philtre into. It was yellowish, wasn't it? About the size of a pinky finger?

There was a tiny yellow bottle in the back. I opened the cork and sniffed. It smelled sweet, somehow, but I could still detect the ginger in it. Maybe the recipe for a love potion on the Internet actually had been for a real love philtre—if you had the magic to make it work.

I took the tiny yellow bottle into the kitchen, then poured

about a third of it into a green-tinged Sprite bottle to disguise it. I put the cap on, then stared at the bottle, trying to see if anyone could tell a difference in color.

Did I have to put in a hair from Branna and something from the guy for a love philtre, too? I didn't know. The sound of Mom's car in the driveway stopped my thinking. I ran and put the bottle of remaining love philtre back in Mom's cabinet, but the kitchen was still a mess when she walked in the front door.

She sniffed the air, then pointed an accusing finger at me. "Have you been trying to make a potion, Izzie?" she asked.

"What if I have?" I said.

Her eyes flickered over the red wine vinegar on the counter. She looked in the garbage can and pulled out the paper I had printed with the recipe from the Internet. "Love potion?" she asked. Her eyebrows rose. "You know this won't work without magic, right, Izzie?"

I shrugged. "I thought I would give it a try. It's for Branna."

"Izzie, Branna is only sixteen. Even if this worked, don't you think it's a little early to try for eternal love?"

"Why? Juliet was only fourteen. Lots of kids fall in love in high school and end up getting married forever."

"But are they happily married? Sixteen seems awfully young. And look what happened to Juliet."

"Branna isn't silly like that. She won't change her mind."

"Oh, really?" asked Mom. "And what about you? If you think a love potion is such a great idea, then why haven't you tried to make one for you and Mark? He's a nice boy, and you love him, don't you?"

I spluttered for a second. Mom really knew how to push

my buttons. "Mom, Mark and I don't need a love potion. We're doing just fine without one."

"It's not because you want to have more time to decide, for the rest of your life? You don't have any teeny, tiny little doubts about whether Mark is the one you will love until the day you die?" There was a flash of pain on her face as she said this, and it made me hesitate.

"Maybe I will do a love potion for me and Mark sometime," I said.

"With that recipe? I won't worry about it, then," said Mom. "Even if you had magic, I don't know that you could make it work. You're never going to be a witch, Izzie."

"Fine," I said, not looking at her. Why did she have to remind me of something so painful? I didn't remember the magical test I'd taken when I was five, but she had told me about it a hundred times. I didn't have magic. I had to live with that for the rest of my life.

"Have you asked Branna about this potion you're making for her?" asked Mom.

"Not exactly," I said.

"What about Mark? Doesn't he know Branna pretty well? Maybe you should ask his opinion of what she'd want."

"Mom, I still haven't told Mark about magic."

"Hmm," said Mom, sounding critical.

"I'm just not ready yet. I haven't found the right moment," I said.

Mom shook her head and started cleaning up the dishes that I had used to make the Internet love potion. She handed me a dishcloth to wipe off the counter. "Don't misunderstand me, Izzie. I like Mark. I just don't think you two are the right fit. He seems . . . well, too steady for you. I'd think you'd be more interested in flash and adventure."

"Flash? Mark is plenty flashy," I said. She should see him on the basketball court. "And I would have thought you'd have had enough of adventure from Dad." It came out hotly, and I knew as soon as I'd said it that it was the wrong thing. But I couldn't take it back.

"Adventure is for the young," said Mom, and left the rest of the dishes in the sink for me to finish up.

After that, I figured telling her about Mel Melot and his wine bottle and the ineffective defense potion would have to wait for another day. Right now, I needed to find a way to give the real love philtre to Branna and the guy she was in love with. Whoever he was.

Chapter 4

The next morning, Branna was at the bus stop, which is between our two houses. She was wearing her tight jeans, which show off how buff she is. She also had on a shirt with pink sequins that I coaxed her into buying a few weeks ago. Just because she's as strong as a guy doesn't mean she has to dress like one.

"Are you and Mark going to the homecoming game this weekend?" she asked me as we found seats in the back of the bus.

"Yeah. You want to come?" Branna usually doesn't like football games, partly because she doesn't like to be around Mark's whole posse. She's shy enough that she'd rather be with a smaller group.

But if she had changed her mind about the game, maybe that was a clue about who she was interested in. Someone in Mark's posse? That would make things easier.

There was Rick Gawain. He's tall enough, but I wondered what they would talk about. Rick doesn't say much; he just grunts when people ask him things. But maybe he's shy, like Branna, and needs to be with a smaller group, too. I was sure I could get Mark to nudge him into asking Branna on a date.

Or there was Will Bishop, student body president. He's not the athletic type at all, but he often has us laughing so hard that we're in tears. A lot of girls were dying to go out with him, and he was happy to oblige. But he never dated a girl more than once. Maybe he was waiting for someone serious, like Branna, to steady him.

"You don't think Mark would mind if I'm there?" asked Branna.

"No, he mostly wants to watch the game. I'm just there as eye candy," I said.

Branna stared at me for a long moment, and I realized what I'd said.

"I didn't mean it like that," I said. "Mark is really great to me, Branna. I am lucky to have him."

"Maybe, but are you a match?" she asked. "Are you destined to be in love with each other? Are you the perfect couple, forever and ever?"

Branna was so serious about everything. Maybe Will Bishop was the right guy for her; maybe he could get her to lighten up.

"I didn't mean anything," I said. "Mark and I are a great match." Although it was nice of her to worry about me like that.

"So what's going to happen next year, when Mark goes to college?"

"He's not planning to go away. He'll be at the Tech," I said. The Tech is here in Tintagel, only two miles from the high school. "So nothing has to change."

"That's what you want him to do? To go to the Tech and hang around here for the rest of his life?"

"What's wrong with that? He doesn't have big plans with his life, that's all."

Branna shook her head. "He should have big plans," she said. "Can't you see that?" Branna had complained more than once that she thought Mark wasn't ambitious enough for me, but I didn't care. I didn't have big plans, either. I just wanted to get a regular job and have a regular life. This love philtre was probably the only magical thing I'd ever be involved in.

"I get it. You don't want a boyfriend like Mark. So tell me what you do want." I could feel the press of the Sprite bottle against my leg as it sat on the floor of the bus.

Name, I thought. *Please give me a name.* "I know you're in love with someone, Branna. The way you reacted when Mel Melot offered you that love potion gave it away. But you've been acting suspiciously for months."

"Suspiciously?" said Branna, going pale.

"Yeah. Unhappy. Moody," I said.

Branna took a deep breath. "Fine. I'm in love. And what do I want? Everything," she said wistfully. "Candles, roses, romance, and eternal love. Romeo and Juliet, Lancelot and Guinevere, Antony and Cleopatra."

Well, those were names, but not exactly what I'd been hoping for.

"Didn't they all die young?" I asked. I don't have much

sympathy for people who think death is romantic. Take it from me: it's not.

"That's not the point. Yes, they died, but everyone dies. The truest lovers live forever in stories."

"Romeo and Juliet knew each other for all of two days. Maybe they would have turned out to hate each other. He probably smelled bad and farted in bed," I said, trying to get Branna to smile.

She didn't.

"My point is that when you fall in love, it's with a real person with flaws. Not with a perfect character from a fairy tale." I wondered why we had never talked about this before. I guess Branna hadn't thought about it until she fell in love, and then she fell hard.

The bus turned and we had to hold on for a minute before we said any more.

"You're saying I should just settle for less than what I want, then?" asked Branna.

"No! I just want you to tell me what you do want." A hint would be helpful in figuring out who to give the other half of the love philtre to.

I didn't know what would happen if more than two people drank it. It might go completely inactive, or it might be—I didn't want to think about that. "Come on. Give me a hint. What kind of guy turns you on? Blond? Dark? Tall? Quiet? Affectionate? Sweet?" When Branna didn't say anything, I added, "Hairy arms? Horns? Pointed ears? Branna, you talk about romance, but you never have any specifics. I'm starting to think you couldn't love a real guy because you have imagined someone so perfect he can't be real."

"He's real, all right," said Branna quietly.

"Then who? Give me a hint. Please."

There was a long moment's pause, and I was afraid she wouldn't say anything. But finally, she said, "He's tall."

"Okay, good." Not Will Bishop, then. Rick Gawain seemed the obvious choice. "What else?" I asked.

She tilted her head to the side and seemed to go into some dreamworld where she could look at his face instead of mine. "He's thoughtful, and brings out the best in everyone around him."

Wait—that didn't sound like Rick Gawain, with his quiet grunting, at all. It was so vague it could be almost anyone. It could even be Mark! But of course, I knew it wasn't.

"And he doesn't know I exist," Branna finished in a whisper.

"Well, I'll have to change that, then. Tell me who it is. I swear I can help you."

"No, Izzie. I'm not telling you a name."

"Is it embarrassing? Branna, tell me you are not in love with the principal or one of your teachers. Or someone who is married."

Branna blushed. It looked good on her; it really did. It made her eyes sparkle and brought out a reddish light in her hair. "He's not married," she said. "And he's our age."

"A junior?"

"No."

I was getting somewhere. "A senior, then." But that still left roughly one hundred guys. I couldn't give the love philtre to all of them.

"Starts with an *A*?" I asked.

"Mmm," said Branna. "No."

"*B?*"

Branna shook her head.

I couldn't go through the whole alphabet before we got to school. We were almost there already. "Well, tell me this, then. You say he doesn't know you exist. Is that in the he-passes-you-in-the-halls kind of way and you have no contact with him? Or is it in the you're-right-under-his-nose-every-minute-of-the-day-and-he-doesn't-think-of-you-romantically kind of way?"

"Right under his nose," Branna admitted, then looked out the window.

Rick, then? We'd see him before school. I would just have to watch Branna and decide if he was the right one. Then all I'd have to do was make sure I got them both to drink the love philtre. How was I going to do that? Well, I'd have to make sure they were really, really thirsty. Maybe at the game?

Chapter 5

After we got off the bus, Branna and I went over to the sunken "pit" in the middle of the Tintagel High commons area, where they had dances. If you really liked someone, you danced down the steps in the pit, because it was crowded there and you had to get close. If you weren't sure, you stayed on the edges. If it was a pity dance, you stayed as far from the pit as possible.

Mark and I always danced in the pit.

We hung out there, too, with his posse. I could see everyone there now, only there was also a new guy I had never seen before.

I'd always thought of Mark as blond, but not compared to this guy, whose hair was white-blond. He had these amazingly blue eyes that looked like they had to come from contact lenses, because that color couldn't be real. He wasn't as tall as Mark, but he seemed tall, the way he drew attention.

And he had this huge, dazzling smile that was like a nuclear reactor compared to Mark's warm, lightbulbish grin.

I hated that smile, and I hated that it made me compare him to Mark. Who did he think he was, smiling at me like that? And why did he seem so at ease? Apparently, this was his first day at Tintagel, but he acted like he was the king of the whole school. I have never liked arrogant guys.

I felt hot with anger and actually had to wipe the sweat from my forehead. I had never been this angry at anyone I just met before. I didn't know why.

"Izzie, there you are," said Mark. He put out an arm and drew me close enough to plant a kiss on the top of my forehead.

I could see the new guy watching, and I could tell he was judging Mark by that kiss on the forehead. But there was nothing wrong with Mark's kissing me like that. There was everything right about it, in fact. It was affectionate, no pressure, a greeting kiss. What more could a girl want from her boyfriend?

I wiped my forehead again and pulled my hair back behind my ears. I wished I had put it up in a ponytail now.

"Izzie, this is Tristan," said Mark.

"Hi," I said, putting my arms tight around my sides, to keep me from accidentally raising them and showing how sweaty I was.

"Good to meet you. I have heard so much about you from Mark." He had a formal way of talking that seemed strange in high school.

"He just transferred from Parmenie," Mark went on.

Parmenie was a fancy private school about fifty miles

away, close to the mountains, with horseback riding and lots of acreage for nature studies. Only really rich kids went there. No wonder he talked like a rich brat.

"Your parents run out of money?" I asked rudely.

"No," said Tristan. Then, a second later, he added, "They died."

That was enough to stop the conversation. I felt like an idiot, and everyone was staring at me.

"I'm sorry," I said, barely getting the words out. "I didn't mean—"

"It was a car accident. Sudden. I'm just starting to get used to it. I knew something had to change in my life, however. So—" He reached out a hand like he was going to brush it against my face, then pulled it back.

What would make him think that I wanted that? Mark was standing right here next to us.

"So he decided to come here," said Mark, patting Tristan on the back. "He's going to run track."

"If I should make the team," said Tristan.

"Oh, you will. I saw you run to the bus this morning. Man, you were fast. I don't think I've ever seen someone run like that before. It was like you went invisible."

Tristan shrugged and then glanced at me.

Invisible? What was going on here? "So, who do you live with?" I blurted out. "Now that . . . ?"

"My uncle," said Tristan. "He's my guardian now."

"Do you like him?" It was a nosy question, but I couldn't help myself.

"He's sufficient," said Tristan.

Sufficient? Why did he say stuff like that?

I tried to imagine living with someone other than my mom, but I couldn't. Why was I being so rude? Maybe he was staring at me too much, but I should feel sorry for him. Instead, I just felt irritable. I wished I could jump in a pool or something. I wasn't on the swim team, though, and I didn't have time for another shower.

I told myself it was just because I was worried about Branna and the love philtre, and that was making me easily annoyed. I took a deep breath and tried to think calm thoughts.

"The one good thing in all of it is that I have learned what's really important in life," said Tristan.

"Like a state championship in track," said Mark, slapping Tristan on the back, "which Tintagel has never had."

Mark cared about stuff like state championships for the school.

I looked over to see Branna focused intensely on the two of them, and then it hit me: Tristan was perfect for her. She wanted someone serious enough to think about eternal love, and Tristan had to be pretty serious after his parents died. He had a long-term perspective, and he seemed strong and sensitive. Plus he hadn't spent the last year ignoring her, like the guy Branna thought she was in love with, whoever he was.

Tristan would be a lot better for her than that guy, and I had just the thing to convince her: the love philtre in my backpack. I could skip all the stuff about trying to find out who Branna was in love with, because that wouldn't matter anymore.

Maybe some people would say that it wasn't my place to

decide who Branna should be in love with. But it wasn't like she was doing a good job of this on her own. I was the one who had the perfect boyfriend, so I figured that gave me the right to make things perfect for my best friend.

Plus I wouldn't have to worry about Tristan giving me that smile. He'd save it for Branna, and that would be quite a relief. I didn't need any temptation close by. Mark was the guy for me.

I didn't think I needed hair or anything for Mom's love philtre to work, just an excuse to get Tristan and Branna each to drink half of the love philtre. It couldn't be that hard, right?

Sure, my mom would say I should tell them what I was asking them to drink, so they could make a choice and all that. But who cared about choice when you could have happiness instead? I could hardly wait!

There would be double dates from now until the day Branna and I graduated from Tintagel High! Tristan and Mark were even friends already, so there would be no conflict between them.

"You going to sit with us at the game tonight?" asked Mark.

"Yes, certainly. That would be ideal," said Tristan. "Who else will be attending?" He was looking at me and Branna.

"Izzie's coming with me, and Branna always goes wherever Izzie does," said Mark. Branna glanced at me ruefully.

"Anyone thirsty?" I asked, and took out the Sprite bottle with the love philtre mixed in. I unscrewed the cap and held it out to Tristan.

"Want some?" I asked, and smiled widely at him.

"I wouldn't wish to take something that belonged to you," he said.

"Don't worry about it," I said. "I can't drink it all myself. I'll get fat. I forgot to get diet this time."

"Izzie?" said Branna. She knows I hate diet soda. I only drink the real stuff, and I don't spend much of my life worrying about getting fat. It's one of the things she and I have in common. We are the size we are, and we don't like to listen to girls who were thin as pencils whine about how many calories a carrot has.

Darn it! I should have thought of something better to say in front of Branna. Now I didn't know how I was going to get her to drink.

"Go ahead, do her a favor, Tristan," said Mark. Tristan shrugged and put the bottle up to his mouth.

I wondered if there would be some visible sign of magic, but I didn't see anything when he tried to hand the bottle back to me. I shook my head. Maybe he hadn't drunk enough of it yet. "Take some more. Please," I said. "I don't want to drink all that."

"If you wish it," said Tristan, staring at me steadily.

Branna hadn't drunk any of the philtre yet, so Tristan wouldn't stare at her lovingly, but maybe he would wander around spouting love poetry at the whole world.

He just stood there.

I was still sweating.

Was it possible that the love philtre wasn't going to work? Maybe it had been sitting for too long in the cabinet and had lost its power—like the potion I'd tried to use on Mel Melot.

I told myself to calm down and wait.

Tristan took a few more sips. "Thanks," he said, and handed back the bottle.

"You don't really like Sprite, do you?" I asked.

"Not usually. I prefer cider or warm milk."

Warm milk? Well, that was different. Not many guys would admit to that.

"And that drink tasted . . . odd. Perhaps it has gone bad?"

"I'm sure it's fine," I said desperately. I couldn't let Branna think there was something wrong with it. I still had to get her to drink it.

"Actually, you look like you just won the state championship," said Mark, nudging Tristan with his shoulder. "You look happy. So the drink can't be that bad, right?"

I looked more carefully at Tristan's face. Mark was right. Tristan sort of glowed, actually—which is what you're supposed to do when you're in love.

Good, good! I held out the Sprite to Branna. "Why don't you have some, too?" I asked.

"No, thanks," she said, staring at the bottle.

"Go on. Tristan's germs aren't going to hurt you. You aren't afraid of cooties, are you?" I teased her.

"He said it tasted off," said Branna.

"There's nothing wrong with it. It's probably just because it's so hot today. That can make things taste different. Heat." I emphasized the word, hoping to use subliminal messages to get her to be thirsty. Mr. Andersson talked about them in psychology, but I'd never had a chance to use them before.

Unfortunately, the messages worked just fine—on the wrong person.

"I think I want some of that," said Mark.

"No!" I froze. He reached for it, and I had a sudden image of Tristan and Mark together—but it was all wrong. Mark wasn't and Tristan wasn't—

Chapter 6

I had to do something quick, so I stepped to the side and turned so that Mark couldn't reach the bottle. Then I chugged down the rest of the love philtre.

"Hey, you could leave me a little," said Mark.

His words only made me drink faster, which caused me to belch loudly afterward. "Sorry," I muttered. Then I thought about what I had done. I had drunk the love philtre. Was I in love with Tristan now? I didn't feel any different.

"Hey, no problem," said Mark. "My girlfriend belches with the best of us." He hugged me; then he swooped in for a kiss.

That was when I knew that Mom's love philtre had worked, and it hadn't needed any hair or anything else.

Because Mark's kiss felt sticky and wet and horrible. I couldn't stand to feel the pressure of his lips on mine, and I pushed him away.

"What is wrong with you, Izzie?" asked Mark, stepping back from me.

"Sorry," I said again, leaning over to catch my breath. It felt like there was an airplane inside my head, taking off and landing over and over again. I was dizzy, and I couldn't keep my balance.

"Must have been that drink," said Tristan. He hadn't been affected the way I had. He seemed perfectly normal, but maybe he was faking it.

"Yeah, I guess. Maybe it really was bad. Do you want me to take you to the nurse, Izzie?" asked Mark. He was being so nice, but I did not want him to touch me.

"No," I said sharply.

"Fine. Whatever," said Mark. He did that sometimes, if I tried to mention I was having my period and felt sick. He did not want to know the details.

The bell rang. "Just go to class," I said to Mark. He didn't argue with me but sauntered off.

Branna hesitated a long moment, looking after Mark and then back at me. "What is wrong with you?" she asked.

"I'm just—" I couldn't tell her the truth. She'd be mad at me.

Maybe the dizzy feeling would wear off soon. There had to be some way to counteract a love philtre. I couldn't be in love with someone I didn't want to be in love with for the rest of my life! That wasn't fair.

I fanned my face.

"Just what?" asked Branna. "You really treated Mark rudely, you know."

I shrugged. "He'll forgive me." He's that kind of guy.

"Yeah, maybe," said Branna.

"I wanted some space, that's all," I said. "What's wrong with that?"

Branna's eyebrows rose. "Fine. Take some Tylenol or something, then. Spare the rest of us the mood." She walked off, books held to her chest.

So I had alienated my boyfriend and my best friend. What next?

"You okay?" asked Tristan. He put an arm around me.

"Yeah, sure. Fine." *Go away,* I thought. *Please, just go away.*

What had I been thinking, sending Branna off? I needed her here with me so she could act as a buffer between me and Tristan.

I did not want to look at him or talk to him. I did not want to think about how nice the place where his throat met his chest looked, or how I wanted to touch the springy hair around his ears, or how I hoped he would hold me like this forever. It wasn't real, anyway. Whatever I felt was just because of the stupid love philtre.

"I think you are not telling the truth," said Tristan. "I think you need assistance."

I had to gather myself. Even if I felt something for him, I could ignore it. I was stronger than any stupid emotional reaction.

"Don't accuse me of lying," I snapped. "It's not nice."

I pulled away from him and breathed deeply. I told myself I was going to get through this. Then I looked back up at Tristan. Bad move. He looked better, more glowing than before. It was not fair. The love philtre made him happy and me miserable.

Tristan said, "Does nice matter so much to you?" He nodded in the direction Mark had gone in.

"Yes, nice matters," I said. "Mark is very nice. That is what makes him such a great boyfriend."

"He left you alone when he could see that you were feeling badly."

"I wanted him to go," I said. "I told him to. He was just doing what I wanted." I was so hot. Maybe I was coming down with something. Maybe I could blame my reaction on a cold or even flu.

Tristan held up a finger. "He was doing what you *said* you wanted. There is a difference."

I held up a finger—my middle finger. But he didn't seem to understand what that meant. I guess they didn't do that gesture at Parmenie or something. Talk about backward. There was no way I could fall in love with this guy. He acted like someone from a hundred years ago.

There were new beads of sweat dripping down my face, and I wiped them away. I'd been sweating even before I took the love philtre, though. I couldn't let Tristan touch me. But he was impossible to ignore. The only thing I could do was make sure that he stayed far away.

"So you're saying that you don't have to listen to what a girl says out loud. Because you can tell what she's thinking? What are you, psychic?"

Tristan shrugged. "I am not a psychic. But I can still tell that you want to be helped."

"Fine. I wanted to be helped. By Mark. Not by you. So go away. Please, go away." I was afraid that if he didn't, I was going to fall on the floor and beg him to kiss me.

Tristan looked confused. Of course he did. I was confused, too. I was late for class, I had just taken a love philtre that was supposed to have been for Branna, and I felt like I was going to throw up.

Hey, maybe that wasn't such a bad idea. I could throw up the love philtre and then it would be like I had never taken it. Maybe I could get Tristan to throw up, too, just in case.

But Tristan murmured something to me in some other language. It sounded like French. It was hard to argue with him when he was speaking in French.

"I will help you," he said in a moment, in English. Then he put his face close to mine. It felt cool and smooth.

I felt the world stop swirling around me. I had never felt so right, so at peace with myself. I had never felt so connected to someone else.

Tristan could have taken advantage of the moment. I felt like I was burning up for him. His lips were soft and thick, just slightly parted.

But he was using them only to talk to me. "How long have you and Mark been dating seriously?"

I did not want to talk about Mark. I answered, "A year or so."

"And how long have you been friends with that . . . other girl?" asked Tristan.

"Most of my life," I said.

"You trust her?"

"Of course. She has never done anything to hurt me."

"Not yet," said Tristan.

"Hey, what's that supposed to mean?" What did he know about Branna? He had met her a few minutes ago.

I turned away from him and picked up my backpack.

"Is this not yours?" said Tristan. He handed me the empty Sprite bottle.

I shook my head. "You can have it." I never wanted to see it again.

"Please, I believe we should speak more openly with each other," said Tristan.

I stared at him. Big mistake.

The love philtre made him look stronger. His muscles weren't larger than they'd been before, really, but they seemed more prominent. He looked like he could leap tall buildings. . . .

I never should have messed with magic.

I turned away from him again and headed for my locker, wondering if I should go to the nurse instead. I really did think I might be sick. But what would I tell her? That I'd taken a love philtre? I didn't think she would have a cure for that.

"Isolde!" Tristan called.

I stopped. I couldn't remember the last time someone had called me by my full name. Even Mom calls me Izzie. Dad was the only one I could remember calling me Isolde, but that was a long, long time ago.

He caught up to me. "There is something between us, Isolde. I think you felt it from the first time you saw me, just as I did. Do not deny it. You and I are the same, both out of place here. We belong together. Can you not see that?"

"I've lived in the same town most of my life," I said.

"That is not what I mean."

"Then what do you mean?"

He rubbed a hand at the nape of his neck.

I liked watching him do that. I wanted to rub his neck myself.

Stop that, I shouted at myself. I wiped a hand across my forehead again, then dried it on my jeans. He looked fascinated.

"I mean that you see . . . things," he finished.

"What, dead people?"

"True things. The true world," he said earnestly, reaching out to touch my forehead.

I flinched.

"The world that has always existed and always will exist, as long as we both—"

I blew out a breath, feeling slightly cooler now. "That's a great pickup line. Did you use it much in Parmenie? How'd it work for you?"

"It's not—" said Tristan.

I put my hands on my hips. "We just met," I said. "And here you are, expressing feelings for me. How real can that be? You are just so cocky that you think you can get away with it with the first girl you meet. Even if she already has a boyfriend who happens to be the captain of the basketball team and the most popular guy in school."

"It must sound strange to you," Tristan said. "But it is not. Truly."

"What do you think Mark would do if I told him about it?" I thought maybe the love philtre was wearing off, because I was mad at Tristan. But every time I looked at him, I wanted to keep looking.

Tristan shook his head. "I can't worry about the conse-quences. I must tell you the truth, whether it is convenient for you to hear it or not."

"Look, Tris," I said, shortening his name in hopes of annoying him. "If I tell Mark about this, he won't let you come near me again."

"I—" Tristan swallowed hard. "Yes. You are correct. I need to remain in your good graces. So what do you wish me to do now?"

I sighed with relief. "Pretend this didn't happen. Pretend you feel nothing for me."

I thought he would argue with me. But he didn't.

He bowed his head. "Fine. I will do my best. But not because what I feel for you has gone away. Nor because it does not matter that you and I are connected in an important way."

He stared at me and I stared back at him, but I looked away first.

I walked off and went to class, though it was the last thing I wanted to do. Arguing with Tristan was almost as addic-tive as thinking about kissing him. I actually found myself missing the feeling of heat I'd had around him. I'd never had that with Mark.

Chapter 7

By the end of school, I felt better. I wasn't feverish anymore, but I went home and lay down for a while, just in case.

Then I took a shower, put on clean, unsweaty clothes, and ate a candy bar (a sure cure for any ills). I also looked on the Internet for cures for a love philtre. Here is a list of them:

1. Death

That was pretty much it. Both of us had to die. If I just killed Tristan, I would pine over his loss, and then I would end up dying of a broken heart anyway. Jumping off bridges, taking poison, or simply refusing to eat and wasting away were some of the top choices for ending the magical power of a love philtre, according to all the old stories, and the new ones, too.

As tempting as it was to strangle Tristan with my bare hands on his bare, bare neck—

Let me put that a different way.

As tempting as it was to poison Tristan from a long distance, it wouldn't really help. I would still be in love with him.

And there was some disagreement on whether even death ended a good love philtre. I read several accounts from people who were sure that they had taken a love philtre in their previous life and were still searching for the one they had fallen in love with then.

I wished I could talk to Mom about it, but she wasn't home, and she would probably just give me a lecture, anyway.

If only she had some secret magic books I could look in. But Mom kept no information about magic anywhere in the house. She's always told me that we have to be ready to leave at a moment's notice, that we can't leave behind any clues about the truth.

The only thing I could really hope for was that I had used the love philtre wrong somehow. I didn't have magic, after all. There might be some loophole, something that would give it an expiration date.

Maybe my sweating and upset stomach were signs that the love philtre had gone wrong and would burn itself out. If so, I just had to live through the worst of it, and then I could go back to my perfect life with Mark. After all, he was the boyfriend I had chosen, and I still loved him underneath all those feelings for Tristan. I just had to focus on that and wait for the rest to go away.

That night, Branna and I drove to the homecoming game in her car. We met Mark and his posse at the ticket booth by the front gate. Except for Tristan, they had all painted their faces purple and gold, Tintagel High's school colors.

I didn't feel hot anymore, which seemed like a good sign.

But when Mark bent down to give me a kiss, I jumped away from him. To cover it, I pointed to his face. "Don't want to be purple and gold," I said.

He shrugged, blew me a kiss, and winked at me.

"Luv ya," he said.

"Luv ya, too," I said with a sigh.

Branna gave me a funny look, but I ignored her.

We went up to our seats, and I sat next to Mark, trying not to touch him, because it made me shudder; clenching my fists; and gritting my teeth. Occasionally I turned and glared at Tristan, who was sitting behind us.

He had promised to leave me alone! He wasn't doing a very good job of it. I could feel his presence there, attracting me, bringing out prickles on my arms and legs.

The cheerleaders were done with their beginning cheers, and our team had gotten a first down. I wished I could focus more on the game, because I actually liked football most of the time. But right now all I could think about was the love philtre and Tristan and Mark.

Finally, Tristan said, "Mark, could I offer to fetch some refreshments for the group?"

"Sure. Thanks," said Mark.

He and the posse dug into their pockets for cash.

Tristan nodded to me and then headed down the metal steps. Somehow, he didn't jiggle them like everyone else did. His feet made a gentle sort of music with rhythm and melody.

I should have turned my attention to Mark, but instead I watched Tristan's backside every step he took from the bleachers to the refreshment stand. It was a nice view. And besides, I was only looking. What was wrong with that?

"Is there some kind of problem between you and Mark?" Branna whispered to me.

I turned toward her but kept my eye on Tristan. "What makes you think that?" I asked, falsely cheerful.

"You haven't said two words to him since you got here. And you're like a porcupine. You won't even let him touch you. Did he do something to make you mad?"

"No, he didn't do anything. I think I'm just feeling . . . sick." I was sick, all right. Sick with feelings for Tristan. It would be so much easier if I just threw myself at him, covered him in kisses, let my body meld with his. . . .

But I was not going to do that. I didn't want that, not really. That was just the love philtre talking.

"Well, you're acting like Mark has the plague," said Branna. "You're going to hurt his feelings."

I knew she was right. I tried to remind myself what had made me fall in love with Mark in the first place.

His deep voice, spoken low, right in my ear.

The way he treated my ideas with respect and always listened to me from beginning to end.

How nice he was to me and to Branna.

How fierce he could be if he thought someone was treating me badly.

Which reminded me that I still hadn't told Mark about Mel Melot. He wasn't at the football game, luckily, but as soon as I could stop thinking about Tristan, I would bring it up.

I thought about the time that Mark had jumped into the pool to save me after one of Branna's swim meets. Someone had thrown me into the deep end, thinking I was on the team. I don't swim, and it could have been a life-or-death situation.

"You know, it seems to me like there is something going on between you and Tristan," said Branna.

"What? I don't know what you're talking about. I was just trying to be nice to him because he's Mark's friend."

Branna's eyes went wide. "Really? Being nice? That's what you think you're doing?"

"He's interesting," I went on. "Changing from his old school to this one after his parents died takes real strength of character. He has been through a lot. You can see it in his eyes, don't you think?" I wished I could see his eyes right then.

Branna muttered something under her breath about me sounding like a Hallmark card.

"Well, he does have strength of character," I said. And strength of legs, and arms, and, well, butt.

This was going all wrong, I thought. I bit my lower lip to try to stop myself from thinking about Tristan, but it didn't work. All that happened was that I thought about Tristan biting my lower lip.

I shook my head. This had all started because I had tried to get Branna to fall in love with Tristan. Maybe that would still work. Not with a love philtre or anything, but with a few well-placed hints. If she fell in love with Tristan, wouldn't that help break the power of the love philtre we had accidentally taken? At least it would be a good cover for me, until

I could fight its power. If Branna was with Tristan, that would make him less tempting. "So, what do you think of Tristan?" I asked. "Cute, isn't he?"

Branna shrugged. "He's a little flaky, if you ask me, changing schools his junior year. Not the most loyal guy ever. It seems like he's just in it for himself, for his own glory."

Of course loyalty would be the first thing Branna would mention. "You think he should have stayed at Parmenie, even after his parents died and he had to move in with his uncle?"

Branna raised her eyebrows. "I would have."

I couldn't contradict that. She probably would have. "But that's just a matter of personal preference," I said. "You can't say you see anything seriously wrong with him, can you?"

We could see Tristan waving from the concession stand while holding up eight cups of soda. He didn't drop any of them, which, if you ask me, showed amazing dexterity and balance.

"He's too blond," said Branna.

"You're blonde," I pointed out. It seemed like Branna wanted to dislike him just because I wanted her to like him.

"He's shorter than I am," she added.

"By a half inch at most," I said. "If you stood together, people probably wouldn't even notice." Plus I bet he was the kind of guy who would tell Branna to wear heels if she wanted to, even if it made him look shorter.

"And he has a big personality," I added.

Branna snorted. "Too big, if you ask me," she said. "He's the kind of person who can't be in a room unless all the attention is on him."

"He's not that bad," I said, although before I took the love philtre, I probably would have said the same thing about him myself. "I think he likes you. He was asking me if you had a boyfriend." Lying in the service of friendship is not a bad thing, is it?

"What did you tell him?" asked Branna.

"Duh? What else? That you were free, and he should be really nice to you because you're a great person."

"And what did he say to that?"

"Well, he's here, isn't he?" I replied.

"He's paying a lot of attention to you," said Branna.

I shrugged that off. "That's just because Tristan knows that you and I are friends. He figures the best way to you is through me."

"What about you? Do you think he's cute?" asked Branna.

"The cutest guy I have ever seen," I replied, for once letting myself say exactly what I thought. "The best-looking guy on the planet, really. I mean, look at his eyes. You could get lost in there."

"Uh-huh."

"And you can't say he doesn't have a good butt. You know what the human butt was made for? Running. And I bet it would be great to watch him run." I would much rather have been at a track meet watching Tristan run than at this football game. Then I bet I could focus on the action on the field!

"Uh-huh," said Branna.

"Plus he has that warm voice, smooth as butter. Don't you think he is someone who falls in love hard?"

"He's not my type," said Branna.

"What? Hot isn't your type? Is that what you are saying?" I asked her, nudging her in the ribs.

"Not that kind of hot."

"You just don't think you're good enough for him. But, Branna, you are." *Please*, I thought, *believe you are.*

"I don't trust him."

"Why not?"

"He's hiding something."

"Branna, he's a great guy. The kind you're always talking about, who falls in love once, and hard. The kind who never gives up." What was I saying?

"Maybe," said Branna.

I heard footsteps coming up the metal steps and I went silent.

"Ladies," Tristan said in a low voice, like a song.

I looked away. Tristan offered Branna one of the sodas, then handed the rest to Mark and his posse.

He ignored me. Finally! I could have kissed him for that. Or not.

Then Branna asked him to sit by her. That was just what I wanted! They chatted for several minutes before the game started again. Branna even laughed once.

And I hated her for it.

I couldn't stop myself, though I was the one who'd tried to get them together in the first place. I didn't like that she was sitting close enough to him that their knees knocked every few seconds. I didn't like that she put her hand on his arm, that she offered him a piece of gum.

I also didn't like that he kept his eyes on her. Or that he stared at her hair and leaned into her when he whispered something.

I wanted to jump between them and kick Branna in the

teeth. I wanted to twist Tristan's arm around his back until he begged for mercy and told me he would never, ever talk to or look at any other girl again.

But I didn't.

Because that was just a feeling. An emotion. Completely irrational, based on a magical love philtre that was going to wear off—soon!

All I had to do was make sure Branna and Tristan fell in love. That was logical and thoughtful and would lead to ultimate happiness in the end. My feelings for Tristan were just a little, teeny, tiny snag along the way.

I stood up. "Excuse me," I muttered. I might want this to happen with Tristan and Branna, but I didn't have to watch it. For some reason, I was starting to drip sweat again. I stood up and told Mark I was going to the bathroom.

"Oh, would you take this to the garbage for me?" Mark asked, and handed me his empty soda cup.

"Sure," I said. I wanted Tristan to fall in love with Branna so I could have Mark all to myself and take all his soda cups to the garbage every day. What a blissful life we would live together once the love philtre had worn off.

Chapter 8

As I walked away and dumped the soda cup, I told myself it wasn't fair to think about Mark like that. He didn't treat me badly. He asked me to do something for him once in a while, and he was usually appreciative—when a game wasn't on.

It had never bothered me before.

Tristan probably wouldn't be a better boyfriend in any real terms. It was just the grass being greener on the other side and all that.

And the eyes bluer. And . . .

I headed down the metal steps and found myself in a crowd of people who were moving toward the concession stand. When I got away, I was in front of the fenced gate that led to the ticket booth. Out in the parking lot was a big black dog. It was running back and forth with frantic, jerky motions, as if it was looking for someone.

I like dogs, though Mom has never let me have one, despite my asking her a million times. And this one was beautiful, with a shiny coat, strong hind legs, and an upright head.

At first, I thought someone had just left it in the parking lot to wait. It wanted to be taken for a run, and now it had to wait, and it didn't understand because it was a dog. Sometimes humans are really cruel.

I went over to the gate and lifted the latch, thinking I would pet the dog. I kept imagining Tristan talking to Branna, and I didn't want to go back to that. I wasn't paying much attention to the dog anymore, or I might have noticed something was wrong.

As it was, I didn't hesitate to open the gate and take a step outside.

"Here, boy," I said.

That was when the dog turned, and I saw that it had two heads. Two heads full of white, shiny, slobbery, gnashing teeth, and a grand total of four eyes. The eyes had a greenish cast to them and stared at me with unnaturally focused interest.

"Uh, nice doggie," I said. I put up my hands and tried to take a step back.

The dog moved quickly, getting between me and the gate. It snapped at my jeans with one head while the other head closed the gate hard enough that the latch fell down and locked in place.

I was trapped now, on the wrong side of the gate.

Stupid, stupid, stupid. All because I'd wanted to pet a dog. Why had I assumed that it would be tame and safe?

"Please, don't hurt me," I said. I could feel sweat trickling down my back. "Please, please."

The head that wasn't pulling at my jeans snarled at me. "Help!" I tried to scream, but my voice came out squeaky.

Then the dog's second head pulled up and stared at me, eye to eye. I was terrified.

Why had I come outside the gate?

If only I still had the potion that I had thrown at Mel. Compared to this dog, Mel seemed like a guppy. I hadn't even told Mom I'd used up the potion or that it hadn't worked, so she had no idea I was vulnerable.

This dog had to be magic. And I had no way to fight it.

I felt a brush of rough fur on my neck and instinctively tried to pull away. But the dog's other head was still clamped on my jeans leg, so I couldn't escape.

"No help," said one head sharply.

If I'd had any doubt that this dog was magic, it was gone then. A talking, two-headed dog? Not likely to be featured on the Discovery Channel anytime soon.

I lifted a hand and tried to wave it at someone—anyone— on the other side of the gate.

But the dog jumped up, letting go of my jeans just long enough for me to take one step. Then it chomped down on my hand.

"No help," it said again with its other mouth, the one not full of my hand.

"No help," I echoed softly. My heart was beating so hard I couldn't hear anything else.

I could feel broken skin, and blood trickling down my

hand. Pain radiated up my elbow and into my shoulder. I could see the imprint of the dog's upper teeth along my little finger. There was blood oozing out of it, but it looked half healed to me already.

How could that be?

I watched for another few seconds as the skin healed up completely. It was bruised, but it wasn't dripping blood anymore, and the pain had settled back into my hand.

How had that happened? I hadn't taken a healing potion.

"Magic," barked the dog. "You magic." It moved the head that wasn't chomping on my hand to my other leg and sniffed it all the way up. Then it sniffed my crotch. And my nearly healed hand. And up my arm.

When it came to my dripping forehead, it stood back on all four legs. "Magic," it said again, in a low snuffle. "Much magic."

"It's not mine," I said with a shaky voice. "It's my mom's." It had to be from her love philtre, unless she had secretly slipped me a healing potion. But why would she do that when she thought I had the protection potion?

"Kill magic," snarled the dog.

Apparently, subtlety was not its strong point.

I kicked awkwardly at the dog's left head and somehow made it let go of me.

I didn't wait for a second chance. I started running and shouting, expecting the dog to chase after me, jump on my chest, and throw me to the ground, then chew into my face. I wasn't going down without a fight.

I ran south toward the school, because I figured the doors would be open, and I knew there was no chance I could open the gate outside the football field in time.

I could hear the dog snarling behind me, could feel its breath on my neck. I screamed, really loudly this time, a death scream, sure my last hope was gone.

There was the sound of something heavy falling behind me.

Don't look back, I told myself. *Just run.*

But I looked back. I couldn't help it.

There was blood splattered all around the asphalt, and the dog didn't have two heads anymore. It had only one head and a stump on the other side, which was quickly dissolving into a regular smooth, one-headed dog neck.

The other head was a steaming lump on the ground, and above the dog was Tristan, holding a sword like you see in movies, with a hilt covered in jewels and a wicked-sharp blade. The way he held it, I could tell that this wasn't the first time he'd used it.

Why hadn't I seen it before? He had to have brought it to the homecoming game.

Sure. Who wouldn't bring one?

I felt myself go cold as a wind kicked up around me.

"Isolde?" asked Tristan. "Are you all—"

He didn't finish, because the dog, now with only one head, suddenly jumped up and came after me. My mouth dropped open to scream again, but no sound came out.

Tristan lifted the sword again and sliced through the second neck.

The head continued its forward momentum. First law of thermodynamics. It turns out that it works with magical creatures as well as regular ones.

The head landed on me, warm and wet, then bounced off and skidded to a stop next to an old Chevy pickup truck.

I was covered in blood and shaking with terror, and I thought I would puke.

Tristan came to my side. "You are safe now," he said. "It's dead."

"Dead," I whispered.

He pulled me against his chest, and I tucked my head under his chin, gasping in the smell of him. It was the only thing that could take away the smell of the dog and its blood. At that moment, I didn't care about anything else.

Chapter 9

With Tristan's arms around me, I gradually stopped shaking. My sweaty forehead was pressed against his neck, but he didn't seem to mind. I felt like I was floating in his arms, and I wasn't sure I ever wanted him to let go. I would have kissed him then and there, but just in time, I heard voices.

I looked up and saw Branna. And Mark. And just about everyone I knew from school.

Mark was running, but he didn't have a weapon. I wondered what he would have done to the dog if he'd come outside before Tristan. Dribbled the two-headed thing like a basketball?

Tristan was the one who had been prepared. He was the one who had saved me. But he was not my boyfriend.

I pulled away from him. "Th-Thank you," I said with effort. He was standing funny, with one side hunched over, but I didn't think much of it.

Mark had his arms outstretched.

Branna's mouth was wide open, her eyes glinting.

Mark reached me. "What happened to you, Izzie? I heard some barking, and I saw Tristan running out the gate. I came right away."

"The—the dog," I jabbered. "It—" I remembered in time that I couldn't say anything about magic. Mom had drilled it into me: never in public. "It attacked me," I said. "It must have been rabid." I could see no sign of the second head on the asphalt now, only the first one. I hoped that meant there wouldn't be news reports about a magic two-headed dog.

"Did it bite you?" asked Mark.

"I—I—don't know," I said, shivering. Suddenly, I was freezing.

"Tristan, did you get bit? Because you might both need shots," Mark said calmly.

I turned to Tristan just as he crumpled onto the ground, unconscious. There was a gaping wound on his side where the dog must have attacked him while my back was turned. I hadn't even noticed it before.

Tristan had held me and whispered assurances to me and made me want to kiss him, and all the while, he'd been seriously wounded. I didn't know if I should love that or hate that about him.

Branna was the first one to reach Tristan's side. Mark struggled with me when I tried to pull away from him. "Let someone else take care of Tristan," he said. "Izzie, you're going to hurt yourself worse if you don't take a rest."

But I wasn't going to watch from a distance as Tristan bled to death. I limped forward.

Branna had pulled off her sweatshirt and was pressing it into Tristan's wound.

Tristan's arms and legs started to jerk, and there was foam coming out of his mouth. This wasn't a normal reaction. The dog's magic must be affecting Tristan somehow.

"Come on, Tristan," Branna said. "Come on. You're going to get through this. You have to live!"

I didn't want her face to be the one he saw when he woke up—if he woke up. I moved to his other side and he seized again.

"That was no ordinary dog," said Branna quietly.

"I know," I whispered back.

"Whatever happened to him, he'll die if he doesn't get treated soon," said Branna.

My eyes were stinging with tears. Tristan had saved me. It was my fault he was hurt. The dog had come to kill me, not Tristan.

"I called the ambulance," I heard Mark say right next to me. Then he put his hand on my shoulder and tried again to pull me back. "Izzie, let Branna take care of him. You need to lie down."

"My mom," I said. "You have to make sure it's my mom coming in the ambulance. He needs her."

"I'm sure your mom is a great ambulance driver, but we want whoever is closest, so they can get Tristan to the hospital as soon as possible," said Mark.

It sounded perfectly reasonable in a world where there was no magic, but my mom would know how to deal with a magic dog's bite. She had healing potions that could do things no doctor could.

I couldn't find my cell phone. I must have lost it in the fight with the two-headed dog. "Call back," I said. "Call back and tell my mom she has to come."

"Izzie, you need to calm down."

I slapped Mark across the face. "Call back!" I insisted.

Mark put a hand up to his face, clearly more in surprise than in pain. "Fine. I'll call back," he muttered.

I leaned forward. "You're going to be all right," I commanded Tristan, who was still unconscious. He was *not* allowed to die on me. He had come into my life and messed up everything. Now he was going to die and leave me alone? No way.

"Okay, your mom is coming," said Mark after a quick conversation on his cell. "She was the one coming in the first place."

"Good." I took a deep breath.

"Branna, tell her she's not going to help Tristan by making herself sick," said Mark.

Branna looked at me. "You're not Tristan's girlfriend," she said bluntly.

"And you are?"

"More than you," she said.

I nodded and stood up. I felt tired, nothing more. Maybe that meant the love philtre really had worn off.

I swayed on my feet, and Mark put out a hand to steady me. "You're burning up," he said. "That can't be good."

Who cares? I thought. It was Tristan who was in danger.

I would have fought Mark, except that I couldn't. I was too weak.

"Branna, there's something really wrong with her," said

Mark. He helped me lie down next to Tristan, and I thought what a good boyfriend Mark was, after I had slapped him and everything. I didn't know what was wrong with me. I just waited while the world seemed to move in waves.

"Izzie?" That was my mom's voice. I could see a kind of blur of her standing over me.

"Tristan," I said. "Help Tristan." He was the one who had gotten bit by that dog.

"He's already in the ambulance. I need you to get in there, too. Can you tell me what happened?" She looked behind her and then whispered, "You can tell me the truth, Izzie. Even if there's magic."

"Dog," I said. "Two-headed. Speaking."

"Two-headed. It was probably a slurg, then. What did it say?"

"Kill me," I said to Mom, desperately holding on to her arm. "Said it wanted to kill me, kill magic."

"Can you tell me anything else about it?" Mom asked.

"Black," I said. "Shiny. Strong."

"How big?"

I tried to lift my hand, but it moved only a little. "Uh—chest high," I said.

"I understand," Mom said.

Then I was being lifted into the ambulance. I could hear something beeping every few seconds, and I thought Tristan must be lying next to me. He was still alive. He was going to make it.

"We'll get you to the hospital," said an EMT.

"Just a moment. I need to talk to her first," said Mom. "She's my daughter." There was a pause. "Privately," she added.

The EMT moved away. Then my mom was between me and Tristan, a hand on each of us. "Izzie, concentrate," she said. "You are burning up. Do you know why? Did you try to use magic?"

I shook my head from side to side, unwilling to admit even then that I had stolen her love philtre.

"Are you sure? I need to know, Izzie."

I hesitated. "Potion," I finally said.

"You took a potion?" Mom asked.

I nodded.

"From home? One of mine?"

I nodded again.

"Well, nothing I have in the house could have caused this response. It has to be something else. We'll have to figure it out later, after you're safe," Mom said. "Listen, Izzie, I'm going to give you and Tristan a healing potion. It will taste terrible, but you have to drink it all. Do you understand?"

"Uh-huh," I muttered.

"And one other thing," said Mom. "I need you to spit in Tristan's potion. And think about him getting better. Think it hard."

"Whuh?" I said.

"I can explain everything later, but I need you to do this now. It will save his life, Izzie, if it can be saved."

It made no sense to me. I wasn't a witch, and I'd never seen Mom spit in her potions to make them more powerful. But I'd save my questions for later.

"Spit," said Mom.

I spat into the bottle she held to my mouth. I saw a flash

of fire, but it disappeared so quickly I wondered if I had imagined it.

Mom certainly didn't say anything about it. She swirled the potion around, then tried to dribble it into Tristan's mouth.

He choked and spat it back up.

"It will help you," said Mom urgently. "I'm a witch. Tristan, listen to me." She tried to pour it in, but he spat it up again reflexively.

"Izzie, you've got to get him to take this. He's slipping fast. Any other human would be dead from a slurg bite. I don't know why he's survived as long as he has already. You're his friend, right?"

"Yes," I said. I was his friend, and more.

"Then you've got to get him to listen to you."

I tried to lift myself up on one elbow, but it was hard. I felt like I had suddenly turned into an elephant but had only a mouse's portion of strength. I would do anything for Tristan, though, even drag my elephant self over to his stretcher and lean close to his ear.

"Tristan," I said. "It's Izzie. Nod your head if you can hear me."

He nodded very slightly and groaned.

"You're sick, Tristan. That dog poisoned you with his bite. You've got to drink something to make you better. Do you trust me?"

"Isol—" He tried to get my name out, but he was drifting in and out of consciousness.

"Tristan, listen to me," I said as loudly as I could. "You've got to drink this. If you love me, if you ever meant anything that you said to me, drink this."

I waited for a second. His eyes fluttered open, and I swear he looked at me and smiled, just like he had when we met. I hated him for that arrogant smile, and loved him, too.

I poured the potion down his throat.

This time, he drank it.

As soon as he was done, I sagged to the floor. I didn't have enough strength left even to get back onto my own stretcher. Mom had to get me onto it, and then she had me drink some of the potion myself.

"Good work, Izzie," she said. "Amazing work, actually. I don't think I've ever met anyone who survived an attack by a slurg." She kissed me and rubbed her cool hands over my hot forehead. "Except your dad."

That was all I remembered for three days.

Chapter 10

"Izzie, I love you," I heard as I dreamed in the hospital. I thought Tristan was saying it, and I was so happy that he was alive.

But when I woke up properly, Mark was sitting beside my hospital bed, holding my hand, and I realized that it had been him all along.

Tristan wouldn't have said *Izzie*, anyway. It would have been *Isolde*.

Mark looked terrible. His face was gray and his beard was in that in-between stage where it didn't look rough; it just looked like he hadn't shaved for three days.

Could it really have been three days? We must have missed the homecoming dance on Saturday night. And I had such a pretty blue silk sheath and red heels that I had planned to wear, with my hair up.

I ran my tongue along my teeth, and they felt like it had been three years since I had brushed.

"Stay with me this time, Izzie," said Mark. "Please, I can't bear it if you leave me." He spoke with a sincerity that I could not doubt. Mark loved me absolutely. He would have been the one to save me if he had been fast enough. Was it his fault that it had been Tristan instead?

"Say something, Izzie. Anything."

"Hi, Mark," I said, because I couldn't think of anything better.

But he seemed happy with that. He closed his eyes and took a deep, shuddering breath. Then he looked at me, his eyes shining with tears. He shook his head; then he spoke in a voice that sounded very small. "I shouldn't let you see me like this. I'll be back in a minute." He let go of my hand.

I pulled him back, surprised that I felt strong enough to do so. I didn't feel like climbing a mountain or anything, but I felt better than I had in the ambulance. "Don't go," I said.

Mark looked down. "I've been waiting," he said. "For days."

"I know."

"Your mom made me go away and sleep a couple of times, but I wouldn't leave the hospital. I slept on one of the couches out there. I wanted to be here when you woke up. I had to tell you that I was sorry."

"It's okay, Mark," I said.

"No. I should have been there for you. I let you go out there by yourself while I was watching a stupid football game. I mean, it wasn't a stupid game. It was an important game for the football team and for the school. But you almost died."

"Mark, you didn't know."

"I know. I should have felt something, though. Don't you think? I knew you'd been gone too long, but I thought maybe you didn't want to come up and watch with us. I was annoyed with you, to tell the truth. Can you believe it? That was the last emotion I felt for you before I heard you screaming."

"Mark, I was annoyed with you, too," I admitted.

"My fault. Can you ever forgive me?" He was getting a little slobbery with tears.

"Yes, I forgive you. I already forgave you. But it was nothing, Mark. I'm fine now, right?" He was being so nice I should have felt loving back. Tristan wasn't even here, but my feelings for him were, and right now they were getting in the way.

"You had this terrible fever for the first two days. They gave you every antibiotic they could think of, but it didn't seem to be doing anything. And then, suddenly, it just started to go down on its own, and now you're awake." Mark patted my hand. Then his hand drifted up to my neck. Then he was kissing me, lightly, on my eyelids and my cheeks and my nose and my chin. Not on my lips, though.

I was kind of glad about that. He was treating me like I was a china doll, so I was able to avoid a full kiss.

I guessed the love philtre hadn't worn off yet after all.

"How is Tristan?" I asked. "Do you know?"

"Oh. Yeah. I think I heard your mother say that he was out of danger. They thought he was going to die the first couple of days he was here. No one knew what was going on with him, but he had multiple-organ failure. Then somehow he just came out of it, about the time your fever went away. They're saying it's a miracle. They were afraid surgery would cause too much trauma, but his wounds seem to be healing just fine now."

I wondered what had happened to his sword. Had he hidden it somewhere, or was it still out there, in the school parking lot? Would people think it was strange and start asking questions, start guessing that magic was involved?

"Can I see him?" I asked.

"Um, Izzie, you just woke up. I sort of want you to myself for a while. Is that too selfish of me?"

There were probably hundreds of girls who would kill to have Mark as their boyfriend, to have him standing over their bedside in the hospital, giving them butterfly kisses. But I wanted to see Tristan. That was all I could focus on.

"He saved me, Mark, and he almost died. I feel like I need to say thank you." Would Mark buy that? I didn't feel like making up an elaborate story. I knew that at some point I would have to tell him the truth, or at least a part of the truth. If the love philtre couldn't be counteracted and it didn't wear off, I might even have to break up with him. But not right now.

"Maybe you could send him a note?" Mark suggested.

I grimaced in frustration. "Mark, I need to tell him in person. Will you go and see if he can have visitors?"

"Now?" asked Mark.

"Yes, please. I can't rest until I see him. You should thank him, too, you know. How would you feel if he hadn't been there for me?"

Mark shuddered and reached for my hand again. "Yeah, you're right," he said. He moved aside and then I saw what was behind him. It was the most amazing floral display I had ever seen. Mark's fitting into the room next to all those vases was quite the engineering feat. They were on a couple of tables, on the floor, on the windowsill, and even on the shelves in the open closet. There were red and yellow and white roses, and tulips and orchids and daffodils, and daisies, and just about everything else you could imagine.

"What are all those?" I asked.

"Oh, they came while you were sick. They're from friends and teachers. The principal. The football team. The basketball team." Mark waved at one vase after another. I was guessing that he had something to do with the teams' sending flowers, but there were still about ten left.

"And the rest?"

He smiled at me like a little kid. "They're mine," he said.

"All of them?" It seemed a bit much.

"Whenever I was afraid you were going to die, or if your mom made me leave the room while they did some treatment, I called up and ordered another one. I didn't want to keep ordering the same thing, because you'd be bored with that. Also, I wasn't sure what was your favorite. So I thought if I got all of them, you'd be happy."

"I'm happy, Mark," I said. I was trying to be, anyway. He'd spent a lot of money, just to show me he cared. I should be wowed.

"I'll go find out about Tristan," Mark promised. He stood up and went to the door. Then he turned back and waved. It was very cute. I really shouldn't care that he had no idea that daisies were my favorite.

He went out into the hallway, and I was relieved.

Chapter 11

There was a knock. "Hi," said Mom, walking in. "I saw Mark come out. Voluntarily. I figured that meant you must be awake. What did you need so badly that you sent him out to get it? I thought you would be glued to him for hours." She made a kissing face.

"Mom!"

"Hey, I remember what it was like to be in love. Just because I'm old—"

"You're not old," I said. "You're just . . ." She looked as bad as Mark, the lines in her face deep and dark. Her hair was mussed up, and Mom never goes out of the house without her hair looking perfect. Also, she had her shirt on backward, but I didn't tell her that.

"I'm just not someone you think about being in love. But I was, and I remember how all-consuming it can be."

I was hoping she would say something about Dad. It would

be the perfect segue into the subject of the love philtre, and then I could find out once and for all if there was anything I could do to counteract it. I didn't want to break things off with Mark unless I was absolutely sure.

But Mom shook her head and didn't say anything else about love. "How are you feeling?" she asked.

"Fine," I said. "Do you know anything about Tristan?"

"I saw him early this morning, about six. That was when he came out of the danger zone."

"Was he really in multiple-organ failure?"

"Yes. Last night."

"You said something in the ambulance, about humans usually dying from slurg bites."

"That's why Tristan was in so much danger. Frankly, I was surprised that he survived long enough for the ambulance to get him to the hospital. If not for my potion and your . . . help, he wouldn't have made it that long."

I held up my hand. "I got bit by the slurg," I said. "Right there." I couldn't even see a trace of it now. "Why didn't I go into multiple-organ failure, too?"

Mom looked away. "You must have a really good immune system."

And Tristan didn't?

Then I thought of something. "Mom, I thought I was running a fever that day. Maybe a cold or something. Wouldn't that have made my immune system worse and not better?" Tristan hadn't shown any of those symptoms as far as I'd seen. And I had felt the first sign of a fever early that morning, when I met him.

"That's interesting," said Mom.

"Did you give me a different potion from the one you gave him?" I asked Mom.

She shook her head. "I gave you both the same strengthening potion."

There was something going on here. Mom was avoiding my eyes.

Was it possible that Tristan had magic and Mom didn't want to talk to me about it? His sword might have been magical. And having magic might have caused a different reaction to the potion Mom had given us both. Or to the slurg. I just didn't understand magic well enough to make guesses.

I would have to think about this later, when I wasn't in a hospital bed. "What about the school? Did anyone else see the slurg, with its two heads? Did they ask questions about magic?"

Mom shook her head. "As far as I can tell, no one saw the two heads. The hospital staff assumes the slurg was just a rabid dog, although the results of their tests on it were rather odd. Hopefully nothing will come from that and we can avoid any direct questions about magic."

I thought that we were safe when it came to Tristan. After all, if his sword did have magic, he wouldn't want it to become public any more than Mom did. But how did I feel about him having magic and me not having it? Did it change anything?

Not really. It just made it more obvious that I belonged with Mark, and I had to get rid of any feelings from the philtre that I had for Tristan.

"And now I have a confession to make, Izzie," said Mom.

I blinked up at her. "Good, because I have a confession to make, too." More than one.

Mom's eyebrows went up.

I figured I would start with the easy one, to see how it went. "About the protection potion you gave me to carry around—I used it up, and I didn't tell you. That's why I didn't have it when the slurg attacked."

"You must have used it on something pretty important," said Mom. "What was it?"

I felt a little silly that I'd thought Mel Melot was the worst thing I had to worry about. I shrugged. "There's this boy at school, Mel Melot, and he was bragging about having magic. He had this wine bottle that never went empty, and he was manipulating people with his magic. You always say that's wrong."

"So you used the protection potion on him?" asked Mom.

"Yeah," I sighed. "I thought he was reaching for something in his pocket, and it was just a spur-of-the-moment reaction. But it didn't work."

"What makes you think that?" asked Mom.

"I thought— You said it was to protect me. In case of danger. But it didn't hurt him at all."

"That potion wasn't supposed to hurt any humans," said Mom. "It was supposed to neutralize magic. And I suspect it did that. Any magic on or near that boy was instantly neutralized."

The magic wine bottle? So maybe breaking it hadn't mattered at all. Or maybe we had been able to break it because of the potion!

"You never told me the protection was just against magic," I said.

Mom sighed. "I wanted you to have a normal life, Izzie. I didn't want you to spend your childhood worried about slurgs coming after you."

I hadn't even known that slurgs existed.

"That's why we came here after your dad died. To get you away from things like that," Mom said.

"I thought we came here because you didn't want me to grow up around people who had magic, because I didn't have any," I said.

Mom went very still.

My mind leaped ahead. "Mom? If I had saved that protection potion for the slurg, would Tristan have needed to help me?"

"I don't know," said Mom. "If I'd taught you properly about slurgs and how to use the potion properly—Izzie, I lied to you. About you not having magic. That's my confession."

"But the test," I said. "The one I failed."

Mom shook her head. "Izzie, you never failed a test. I made that up. I was trying to protect you, but it may be that I put you in even more danger—" She cut herself off.

I didn't fail the magic test? All this time, I'd thought I would grow up normally, graduate high school, go to college, maybe get married someday. Be Mark's girlfriend, because what else was there for me to do if I didn't have magic?

And now—

The slurg had said it smelled magic on me. I'd thought it was the love philtre. But why had I healed so quickly? Was that because of my own magic?

"You lied to me," I said.

"How much do you remember about your dad dying, Izzie?" Mom asked.

"I remember being sick, and Dad was sick, too. And you gave me a potion, but Dad died before you could give it to him, too."

Mom stared at me. "What do you really remember?" she asked.

I hesitated for a long moment. "A dream," I said. "A huge serpent with scales who devoured people and other creatures, fairies and mermaids and such, just for their magic. And I remember feeling so hot I thought I would burst into flames. And Dad—he was hot, too. I thought that was because he had a fever."

"I let you believe that because it was easier," said Mom.

"He didn't die from a fever?"

"No, sweetheart."

I thought of the slurg, which had been an evil, magical creature sent to destroy me. "That serpent?" I said. "It was real?"

Mom didn't say anything. The answer was in her eyes. "When your dad died, you had just used magic for the first time. You didn't know much about it. You only used it accidentally. I thought telling you the truth would be dangerous. So I told you that you didn't have magic, and I did everything I could to make sure you didn't realize I was lying. I wanted to make sure your dad's enemy—and his servants—couldn't trace your magic scent."

I couldn't believe it. My whole life I had believed that I had no magic, that I would have to live in the regular world. And it was a lie?

"You have to understand, Izzie. You were five years old. You were so small. I always knew I would have to tell you the truth when you grew up. I was just waiting for the right time. But it never seemed to come, and you seemed so happy thinking you didn't have magic. I started to wonder if you didn't want to remember it, after what happened to your dad. Then you made up that love potion, and I began to wonder—"

"So I used magic to heal myself after the slurg attack?"

Mom shook her head. "That's not what your magic does. And besides, you had to use it before the slurg came. That's how it tracked you, through your magic." She closed her eyes for a moment, and I wondered how I had healed myself. "But that's not what we need to think about right now," Mom said.

It wasn't? "What, then?"

"Izzie, the slurg is the least powerful of the minions that the serpent will send after you, now that it knows the scent of your magic."

"The least?" I said.

"I need to prepare you as soon as you get out of here. I'll make some potions for you, and—"

"Mom, don't you think it's time you taught me how to make my own potions?" I asked.

"Oh, Izzie, you can't make potions," said Mom.

"Why not?"

"You're not a witch," she said. "You never have been."

"Then what am I?"

"You're an elemental sorceress. You take after your father. Your magic is different, more powerful than mine and maybe than his. That's why they are after you, the slurg and the rest. I will tell you all about it as soon as we get home."

I thought about the other confession I had to make. Compared to what Mom just told me, it seemed insignificant. She couldn't get mad at me about the love philtre, not after what she had done.

"Mom, you know that love potion from the Internet that I was working on?"

"Yes," said Mom. "The one you said was for Brangane?"

"It *was* for Branna," I said. "But—it's complicated. I ended up taking it. And so did Tristan."

"Hmm," said Mom. "Well, luckily, it was a bogus recipe, especially without a witch to put in her magic."

This was the hard part. "Mom, I sort of figured it wasn't going to work. So I dumped it out: The recipe from the Internet."

"Nothing to worry about, then," said Mom.

"Well, except that what I drank—and Tristan, too—was your love philtre. The one you left in the cabinet from that wedding. Remember?"

Mom's face went white. That seemed like a bad sign. "You took my key, opened my cabinet, and stole one of my potions?"

I don't think I had ever seen my mom angry before. I'd seen her crying for Dad, for people who died in her ambulance. I'd seen her frustrated by politics, but never truly angry. Her eyes were strangely dark and unfamiliar.

"I'm sorry," I said. "I really am."

"Which one did you take?" Mom asked.

"The one in the yellow bottle. It smelled a little of ginger."

Mom didn't say anything for a moment, but her eyes seemed to go normal again.

She stood up and shook out her hands. "Well, thank goodness for that."

"For what?" I said, surprised.

"For you not understanding my potions."

Huh? "What didn't I understand?"

"Next time, maybe you will think twice before stealing my potions and trying to use them without any instructions. Or trying to use any other magic you are not trained in, for that matter," said Mom.

"Okay," I said. "So can you deactivate the love philtre?" That was what I wanted, wasn't it?

"No," said Mom.

"Then . . . what can you do?"

"A properly activated love philtre is impossible to change," said Mom. "You know that, Izzie. We've talked about love philtres before, and how dangerous they are. No one should ever be forced to take one against his or her will, precisely because they cannot be reversed. Once you are in love because of a love philtre, it is forever."

"But—Mark—" I said. "He's the one I love. He's my real boyfriend."

"Too bad," said Mom cruelly. She was watching me, and it was almost as if she was enjoying this. "You shouldn't have played with magic you didn't understand, Izzie. I hope you've learned a lesson you won't soon forget. Magic can be dangerous."

"But, Mom—this is real life. This is about Tristan, and Mark. And me."

"I know what it's about. Better than you do, I think." Mom stared at me, her arms wrapped around her shoulders.

"So I'm going to be in love with Tristan forever?" I asked.

"What do you think?" asked Mom.

"I wish—Mark doesn't deserve this."

"No, he doesn't. But life is hard," said Mom. "Especially when you're sixteen."

That was not what I wanted to hear.

"You need your rest, Izzie. I'll come back and talk to you later. Maybe I can find Brangane and bring her in."

"Oh, is she here?"

"She's been here almost as much as Mark has," said Mom.

"With Tristan?" I asked, jealous.

"No. In the waiting area."

Good, I thought fiercely.

Mom went out the door, leaving me thinking about Tristan and magic. I'd never told Mark the truth about Mom's magic. Maybe that was because a part of me knew I had magic and I didn't want to tell him that, either. I wanted to be unmagical and to live an uncomplicated life with him. Or I had, until I met Tristan.

Chapter 12

Someone brought me a tray of food—mashed potatoes and gravy, I guess. It was kind of hard to tell, it was so colorless.

Then Mark came in, walking gingerly around the flowers. He looked good, like he'd shaved and splashed water on his face and hair. Just not as good as Tristan.

He put a hand on my arm and leaned over the bed. "I was afraid I'd dreamed you'd woken up."

"No dream," I said, and let him hold my hand for a few minutes. This love philtre was a real pain. It made me feel tense around anyone but Tristan, and I hated the way I was treating Mark.

When my arm felt like ants were crawling up and down it, I faked a coughing fit and pulled my hand away from Mark to cover my mouth.

"Are you all right?" he asked. "Should I call a nurse?"

I wrapped my arms around my stomach. "No, I'm fine. Really."

"But if you get a cold or something now, it could be bad. Your immune system is down. They should give you antibiotics and stuff," said Mark. He batted a drooping daisy out of the way; then, when it flipped back on him, he turned around and snipped it off.

I watched sadly as Mark threw the happy-faced flower into the waste basket by my bed. "Antibiotics aren't for colds," I said absently. "A cold is a virus and an antibiotic only helps with a bacterial infection. Plus, they already gave me plenty of those."

"Well, there must be something they can give you," said Mark stubbornly. "I should go wash my hands. I washed them before I came in, but maybe I picked up some germs along the way." He went into the bathroom, and I heard him scrubbing away. When he came back, his hands looked red and raw.

"Maybe I should wear a mask and some gloves," he said. "To make sure you don't get sick from me. I don't know what I would do if I found out I was the one who made you stay in the hospital longer." He looked so pathetically anxious. His dark blond hair had fallen into his eyes, and I remembered how much I used to love those brown eyes.

"I'll be fine," I said. I wondered who felt guiltier right now, Mark or me.

It was really all my fault. I was the one who had decided to use magic to help Branna. I was the one who drank the love philtre. I was the one whose magic had called the slurg. But I couldn't tell him any of that.

I knew I was going to have to break up with him. It wasn't fair to feel the way I felt for another guy and keep Mark as my boyfriend. Mom said there was nothing I could do to reverse the love philtre, so I had to accept it. I wasn't going to be able to put my arms around Mark's neck while he bent over and put his arms around my waist. I wasn't going to see his eyes light up when he saw me across the room. I wasn't going to feel his big hands brush against my cheeks.

Unless . . . What if Tristan had an answer? He had survived the slurg attack against all odds. He had used that sword, and he obviously hadn't been surprised to see a two-headed, speaking dog. Maybe he knew things about magic that Mom didn't know. After all, it had been years since Mom had been around other people using magic. There could have been discoveries made, new inventions, new potions. I wasn't going to give up on me and Mark yet!

"So how is Tristan?" I asked. "You saw him, right?" As soon as I mentioned his name, I could feel the blood pulsing at the base of my throat. I had never felt like this about Mark. I didn't know if I ever wanted to feel like this about anyone. It wasn't comfortable. It was downright frightening.

"Yes. I went to see him, just like you asked. He's awake, and they were talking about letting him have some food, too. It looks like he's doing as well as you are now." Mark smiled.

"Good. Thanks," I said. That was all the attention I could spare for Mark. I could see Tristan in my mind, his blue eyes, his bulging biceps, his megawatt smile. "When can I see him?" I asked. My whole body was throbbing now. One thing that had been good about being unconscious—I hadn't felt this desperate about Tristan then.

"Maybe tomorrow, they said."

"Why not today?"

"Well, I didn't ask. But Tristan isn't ready to get out of bed. And I don't think you are, either."

"Get me a wheelchair," I said. Simple, right? I waved him toward the door.

"Uh, I don't think that's a good idea." Mark rubbed his chin. "Izzie, you almost died, and so did he. You're both still recovering. Exposure to the germs outside this room could be bad for you."

"This is a hospital, Mark. How many germs can there be here? I'm sure I'll be fine." I did not want to lie on this bed arguing with him—not when I could be with Tristan.

"Let me go talk to the nurse," said Mark, heading for the door.

"No!" I lurched out of bed to stop him. It was like being on a ship at sea, except I was the sea. I couldn't find my footing.

Mark reached for me, but I sagged into the chair beside the bed.

"Go. Get. A. Wheel. Chair," I panted.

"Izzie, you're not thinking straight," said Mark. "I have to do what's best for you here."

I looked him straight in the eyes, and I saw him flinch. "I want you to get me a wheelchair and take me to Tristan's room. I need to thank him for saving my life. It will take five minutes. It seems like the least you can do for me, after all I've been through."

I felt horrible manipulating him like that. But what else

could I do? I had to see Tristan. It was for both of us, not just for me.

"I could figure something else out, maybe," said Mark. "A video feed with computers and webcams." Mark had always been good with technology.

I gritted my teeth and tried to remember that I had once loved Mark with all my heart. I wanted to again. As soon as I fixed things with Tristan. "I need to see him in real life. He didn't save my life on a screen, after all."

"Well—" said Mark.

"You're the one who will be doing the work, Mark. I just have to sit in the wheelchair while you push me around."

"But Tristan—"

"He won't be getting out of bed, either. And it's not like I'm going to infect him with anything." Still, I wasn't sure I could keep myself from kissing Tristan, even if Mark was there. I would definitely have to make this a private conversation.

Mark brushed a hand across my face, to push my hair out of my eyes.

I backed away.

"What?" he asked.

"Just get me to see Tristan." I knew I sounded angry. I was angry. But not at Mark. Mostly I was angry at the love philtre.

Mark sighed. "If that's what you want me to do, I'll do it. I think it's crazy, but I guess that's what I love about you. You've always been a little crazy." He smiled gently, which only reminded me of Tristan's bigger, better smile. It was not fair to Mark, but that was the way it was for now.

• • •

Mark left the room to look for a wheelchair. While he was gone, I fidgeted. Then it occurred to me that I was going to see Tristan soon and I had no idea how I looked. I had been asleep for three days. Before that, I had been slobbered all over by a magical two-headed dog. It couldn't be good.

I lurched toward the bathroom and looked in the mirror. It wasn't too bad. I smoothed out my hair with my fingers and washed my face. I found a toothbrush and toothpaste in a bag below the sink. I had never brushed so hard in my life.

When I was done, I looked at myself again. Maybe if I had some makeup? I could ask Mark to go get it for me. Would that be too much of a giveaway, me wanting to look good for Tristan but not caring about what Mark thought?

Just then, Mark came back in with a wheelchair. He looked behind him. "Okay, let me help you get in here."

I knew he would try to touch me again, so I acted like I was fine. I was woozy, but I pretended to be steady and was sitting in the wheelchair in no time.

"Are you sure about this?" Mark asked.

"I'm sure, I'm sure. Will you get on with it?" I said, irritated with the delay.

Mark opened the door and checked up and down the hallway. "There are two nurses talking. Let's just wait a few minutes."

I tapped my fingers impatiently.

"Okay, they're gone. Are you ready?" asked Mark after a few minutes.

"Yes," I hissed at him.

He pushed me to the door. "He's down this hall, and up the elevator," whispered Mark. He didn't have to tell me! He just had to get me there!

We had made it halfway down the hall when Mark suddenly pushed me into an empty room. "Nurse!" he warned me. In a few minutes, he pushed me out again and into the elevator. "Whoo! That was fun. You always make me feel like I'm alive."

That made me feel terrible. Maybe I should just let him down easy and give up trying to end the love philtre. But it was all so complicated. Anyone who thought magic made things easier had never used magic.

Luckily, we got to Tristan's room without further incident. Tristan was asleep, but as soon as I saw him, I wanted to touch him. Mark pushed the wheelchair close to the bed, but I inched it even closer with my feet.

"You can go now," I said curtly.

"You sure you'll be okay?" said Mark.

"I think Tristan has already proved he can protect me," I said.

There was a long silence.

I could have tried to take it back. On the other hand, maybe it was for the best.

"Yeah," said Mark slowly. "Call me when you need me," he added as he closed the door. "If you do."

As soon as Mark was gone, I focused all my attention on Tristan. He looked sort of yellow, and there were bruises up and down his face, neck, and chest. Maybe below that, too, but I didn't peek beneath the hospital gown, however tempted I might have been.

"Tristan?" I whispered. I put a hand on his arm.

"Isolde," he said in that beautiful baritone voice of his. Then he opened his eyes and started. "Are you real?" he asked.

"I'm real," I said. "I'm right here."

"You did not die."

"No. You saved me. Don't you remember?" Hadn't anyone told him? Maybe he hadn't been awake enough.

"I remember, but I was afraid it was a dream, what I wished had happened. I also remember the slurg eating you, and me coming to you too late. They are very vivid memories, I assure you." His crisp way of speaking made me melt.

I wondered about the strange language he had spoken on the day we'd met, not even a week ago. The sound of those words had been so sexy. Maybe I could get him to do that again later.

"We're both alive. We're in the hospital. They thought you were going to die."

"You saved me," he said. "I can taste your magic on my tongue."

Don't go there, I thought. *Don't make me think about your tongue.* Just being next to him was hard enough.

"It was my mom's magic," I said. "She gave you a healing potion in the ambulance." But I remembered she had also asked me to spit into it. At the time, I hadn't thought I had any magic of my own. "I need to talk to you, Tristan. About why you think you love me."

"Yes?" His eyes were very wide.

This was my last chance. "I gave you a love philtre. Do

you remember that drink? The Sprite bottle on the day we met?"

"Yes," said Tristan. "I remember."

"Well, it had magic in it."

"Yes. I knew that. I could smell it."

What? "Why did you drink it, then?" I remembered now that he had said it tasted off.

"It was from you. I trusted you," said Tristan. "I knew any magic you used could not be bad, my love."

"Don't call me that."

"I am sorry," he said, looking away.

He was so adorable when he did that! It was hard to have a normal conversation with him when I wanted to smother him with kisses. But we had to be sensible here. "I brought it to school for Branna."

"Brangane?" said Tristan, pronouncing it differently, as three syllables instead of two. "The tall one who believes she can still be your friend?"

Whatever that meant.

"The tall one who could kick your butt," I said. "And she needs a boyfriend. So I saw you and thought you were cute enough, and maybe you would be a good match."

"Hmm," said Tristan. Obviously, he did not think it was a good idea.

I didn't really think it was a good idea anymore, either. Branna needed someone more even-tempered. Someone like—well, I would worry about that later. Although maybe I should have learned my lesson about love philtres at this point. "Anyway, what I am trying to ask is if you know how to reverse a love philtre. Nothing against you," I said. I licked my lips and couldn't stop myself from wishing I could lick his. "But I think people should fall in love out of their own free will." Did I sound like my mother?

"Love philtre. But there was no love philtre," he said. "That is not why—"

"It is why," I interrupted. "Look, I thought maybe you knew something new about magic, about how to counteract a love philtre. Haven't you been around magic all your life?" Unlike me.

"Well, yes," said Tristan. "But—"

"Then tell me about love philtres," I said.

"A true love philtre can never be counteracted," said Tristan, his face a study in earnestness.

I sighed. "Then it looks like we're stuck with each other, at least for a while." I had no reasonable expectation of breaking the love philtre now, but I clung to the hope anyway. At the same time, I was on fire for him. I could literally feel my temperature rise now that I was in the room with him.

"They will keep coming," said Tristan, his hand outstretched. "You must know that."

I jumped when he touched me. Then I grabbed his hand and rubbed it back and forth against my cheek. "Who?" I said absently. Maybe Mark had been right. If I wanted a rational conversation with Tristan, I should have it remotely.

"The servants of your father's enemy," said Tristan. "Like the slurg. Your father was very powerful. When you were born, they wanted to kill you while you were young and weak, not yet ripe in your magic. Your father protected you. But then he died and you and your mother disappeared, cut off from all contact with the magical world. No one could find you. Many have sought for you, moving from place to place in hopes of discovering you."

Tristan had come from the magical world because he was looking for me? Was it luck that had brought us together, or something else?

"Now that you have used your magic, however, they will be able to find you," said Tristan.

"What did I do with it?" I asked. I still didn't know.

"The day I arrived at Tintagel. You were on fire with it. I knew I had found you the moment I saw you. I thought you meant for me to see. You are using it now. Did you not know?"

"I am?" Could I turn it off? I felt hot. Was that magic?

"Your magic calls to me," said Tristan. His gaze was intent on me, and I groaned and got out of the wheelchair. The pain of standing was nothing compared to the pain of not kissing him. I pressed against him on the bed and felt his lips against mine.

I think I went unconscious after that, or maybe I was delirious with happiness.

The next thing I knew, Tristan was talking again, and my head was nestled next to his on his hospital bed.

"You are the one who will save us," said Tristan.

"What?"

"You will save us. I know it is true. You will free us from the serpent who enslaves us. We have been waiting for you."

"Who are you talking about?"

"I will show you," said Tristan. "They will be eager to see you. When you are ready, of course."

"Ready for what?"

I heard a knock on the door and leaped away from Tristan and back into the wheelchair, just in time, because Mark walked in. "You okay? You look tired," he said.

"Yeah, I'm tired," I said.

"You ready to leave now? I was worried you had been in here too long."

Was he suspicious? He didn't seem to be. He was the kind of boyfriend who trusted his girlfriend completely, and it was unfair that I wasn't a better girlfriend. I would have been, but then the love philtre got in the way.

"I'm going to wheel her out now," said Mark. "I really do appreciate everything you did for her, Tris." He shook Tristan's hand firmly.

I stared at the two hands, one pale, one darker. But it was the pale hand I thought about once I was back in my own room.

Chapter 13

Mark helped me back into bed. "I love you so much, Izzie. I just want you to get better so we can be together again, all right? I'll be here for you."

It was cowardly of me, but I pretended to drift off to sleep. Mark stayed with me, sitting at my bedside. When he tried to touch me, I rolled over or groaned. I didn't want to deal with him now.

After what seemed like forever, Branna came in. "How is she?" Branna whispered.

"I think she's going to be okay," said Mark.

I heard the scrape of a chair and the sound of Branna sitting down next to Mark. I was suddenly curious about what they were going to say about me. And you know what they say about eavesdroppers.

"You can't blame yourself for this," said Branna.

"Of course I can," he said. "I let her get attacked by a rabid dog, and I didn't even know she was in trouble."

"She was the one who walked out of the game," said Branna.

"And I asked her to take my garbage for me. That was the last thing I said to her."

"You asked her to do something nice for you, and she agreed. What's wrong with that? If she didn't want to do it, she could have said no." Branna sounded hostile.

"I must have done something to make her mad," said Mark. "I wasn't paying enough attention to her. Isn't that what girls always say about their boyfriends? That they become complacent and stop doing all the little things that made their girlfriends fall in love in the first place?"

Mark is the kind of guy who would know something like that. He probably read a book about how to treat a girlfriend.

"If she's not in love with you anymore, it's not because of you, Mark," said Branna. What was she doing?

"It has to be," said Mark desperately. "Because if it's not, then I can't fix it. And I have to be able to fix it. Tell me what she wants, Branna. You know her better than I do. I'll do anything."

Branna sighed.

"Please tell me. You don't hate me, do you, Branna?"

"I don't hate you, Mark," said Branna.

"Then what should I do? Or what should I not do?"

There was a long pause. I could have pretended to wake up then, but I didn't. I wanted to hear what Branna would say. I had made the love philtre for her because I wanted her to be happy. I thought we were best friends, but she wasn't acting like it now.

"If you really want to know, I think maybe you hover too much," said Branna. "You make her feel smothered. You should give her some space."

Okay, that wasn't bad. Branna was giving good advice to Mark. I never should have doubted her.

Mark groaned. "I should have known. She feels like I'm hanging on her all the time, doesn't she? Branding her as mine or something. I just like being with her, and I like to touch her."

"Not every girl would dislike that," said Branna. What was that supposed to mean?

"I know, but this is Izzie," said Mark. "What else?"

"Well, you could ask her about her dreams in life. What she wants to do after high school."

Mark had never asked about that. And I was glad, because I didn't know what I would tell him. Mom always said that I should wait and see, that I might change my mind about what I wanted to do when I was older. Now that I knew I had magic, I could see why she had said that. Magic changed everything.

"I never thought of that. She must think I'm an idiot. Anything else?" asked Mark.

There was a long silence.

"I can see you're thinking of something, Branna. I know that look in your eyes."

"Really? I sort of thought you didn't even see me, Mark. I'm just Izzie's friend, the background music. The wallpaper. The ditto." She sounded bitter. I had heard that tone in her voice before, but I thought she was just jealous that I had a boyfriend.

"You're not forgettable, Branna. I see you. I just don't want to . . . you know, overstep the line. I have to keep Izzie as my top priority."

"Is that what you're doing?"

"You're very pretty, Branna. Is that what you want me to say?"

"I don't want you to say anything. Not if it's a lie."

"I'm not lying to you," said Mark. His voice was a little hoarse.

"No? You just want to make sure I tell you what I know about Izzie."

"That's not—" Mark began. "Okay, that is true," he said, correcting himself. "But I'm not lying. I do think you're pretty."

"Just not as pretty as Izzie."

"You and Izzie are pretty in completely different ways. She's . . . well, she's like a little spark in the darkness, like a star on a moonless night. And you're like the sunshine, Branna."

What was he saying? She was like sunshine? That didn't sound like the kind of thing you'd say to your girlfriend's best friend.

"Really?" said Branna.

"I think it's a shame that you don't have a boyfriend already. I guess I figured you were still looking. But if you want me to whisper something in an ear, I'm sure I could get Will or Rick to take you out. Or Mel."

I tried to calm down. If he was suggesting Will or Rick,

that meant he wasn't thinking about Branna in any romantic way. Although, really, did I have any right to look down on him if he was?

Yes, I decided I did. If I had fallen in love with someone else, it was because of a love philtre. Mark had no excuse. Neither did Branna.

"No, please don't do that. I don't want to go out with them." Branna's voice was soft and trembly.

"Is there someone else? Tristan?" asked Mark.

"No, not him, either."

"Well, if you see someone you like, just give me the word. I have my ways."

"Thanks for the offer," said Branna. "But I'd rather date someone who chooses me for himself."

"I guess I can understand that."

Another pause. At least Branna was consistent, I thought.

"One other thing about Izzie," said Branna.

"What is it?" Mark asked eagerly.

"You should find out more about her mom and dad."

My mom and dad? Why was Branna telling him that?

"I thought her dad was dead," said Mark.

"He is dead, but she loved him a lot. I don't think she talks about him much with anyone. She needs to, though. He was her mom's one true love, and you could get some real insight into how Izzie thinks about true love by listening to her stories about her parents."

"Her dad. That makes sense. Branna, thanks." Mark sounded relieved, happy. Just the way he should.

"And about her mom, you should watch her sometime.

Or talk to her about her work. She's not just an ambulance driver. She has other . . . talents."

Was Branna trying to out my mom's magic? She didn't know about my magic, though. I hadn't told her yet.

"Izzie must think I am completely blind, that I'm missing out on so much of her life. I'm glad I've had this chance to talk to you, Branna. You are the best girlfriend ever. Uh, I—I mean, the best girlfriend of my girlfriend," Mark stammered. "Not *my* girlfriend, of course. I didn't mean anything like that."

"I know," Branna sighed. "I think everyone knows that I'm not your girlfriend or anyone else's."

I guess I had been pretty clueless about Branna. The only excuse I had was that it seemed everyone else—Mark and the rest of the posse—had been clueless, too. The only one who had guessed was Tristan. He'd said that Branna believed she could still be my friend. And now I could see that was hard, because Mark was between us.

Chapter 14

The next day, the doctors let me go home. They were surprised I was ready so soon. I had missed almost a whole week of school and the homecoming dance, and my world had changed completely. I had no idea if I could go back to high school as if nothing had happened, but I was going to try.

On the drive home, Mom told me that Tristan would most likely be home the next day. I hadn't been able to talk Mark into bringing me to see him in the hospital again, so I had to depend on Mom for all my information. She kept hinting that I should break up with Mark, but I ignored her. I wasn't ready for that yet, and I still wasn't sure about Branna. She had visited me later the previous afternoon, and we had talked about everything but Mark and Tristan. If I was really unselfish, maybe I should just push her and Mark together. I guess I wasn't that unselfish.

When Mom and I got home, the first thing I did was lie on the couch in the front room with my eyes closed.

"Are you all right? What's wrong?" Mom came over to check on me. "Are you having a relapse? Should I take you back to the hospital?"

I opened my eyes and smiled at her. "I just wanted to smell home," I said. "You don't know how awful it was in the hospital all these days."

"I don't know how awful it was? I think I know it just as well as you do," said Mom. Then she closed her eyes and took a sniff, too. "It does smell . . . normal, doesn't it?"

Well, normal for our house, anyway. It smelled of ginger and vinegar and something else. Maple syrup, maybe? "What have you been making?" I asked. It couldn't be another love philtre, could it?

"An invincibility potion," said Mom. "It was all I could think about while you were in the hospital."

"I didn't know there was such a thing," I said.

Mom looked away. "Well, it's not completely impervious to magical power. But it works against almost everything. When your dad and I were—well, when we talked about the serpent and his going against it, I tried to make this potion, but it was a complicated recipe, and I kept getting it wrong. So he went to the serpent without it."

She took a deep breath and shook her head. "I have been working on it ever since then, trying to perfect it. I think it's almost there. But we can talk about that later. Right now, I want you to rest."

I settled back on the old couch with the lumpy cushions. We'd never had new furniture that I remembered; it was all secondhand. Mom was careful with money. What she made, she spent on the house and our car and food. And her potion ingredients. I couldn't remember the last time Mom had bought anything for herself. She just made do. It used to annoy me, but I was starting to understand why the potions were so important.

After a half hour, I went up to my room. I lay on my bed and stared at the glow-in-the-dark stars that Mom had put up on the ceiling when I was five. They were supposed to help Dad find me from heaven. I remembered being so worried about that back then. But I hadn't looked up at the stars in years.

Suddenly, I remembered something else I hadn't looked at for a long time. I got off the bed and went to the bookshelf by my desk. Underneath a bunch of overdue library books and some papers from fourth grade, I found my old photo album. It was just big enough for a few small pictures of me with my dad.

I teared up as soon as I saw the first one. It was me as a newborn baby, on my dad's stomach. He had his hand on my back, and I had my eyes closed. The look on his face is hard to describe, not a smile, but pure contentment, like he had found out what life was all about. And it was me.

No wonder I had always liked that picture. It made me feel safe and secure. That is, it had until I got old enough to realize that Dad had died anyway and that he was never going to be there for me now. That was when I had stopped looking at the photos.

I turned the page to the next picture. I was taking my first steps, and Dad was holding out his arms to me. I remembered him telling me about the picture. I could almost feel him beside me again, whispering in my ear, his voice soft and low. "You were scared to walk. You were almost fourteen months before you even tried. And you would only do it for me, Isolde. You wouldn't even look at your mom while you were standing. But when I held out my arms, you would toddle toward me. And I would step back, and you would keep coming, on and on until you realized that you didn't need me after all."

I had needed him. I still needed him.

Me in the bathtub with Dad pouring water on my head.

Me feeding myself birthday cake with my fingers.

Me blowing out candles at my third birthday party.

Dad and me mixing up mac and cheese, which used to be my favorite food ever.

My first day in kindergarten in the magic world: I still remembered the backpack Dad had bought me, red as fire. I remembered how he and I had picked it out together, and he had told me that I'd made a good choice, that red was a good color for me. I'd thought he meant something more, but I'd never known what.

And then the photos ended. Dad had died in February of the year I was in kindergarten. Now all I had left of him was this album.

Wearing an apron and smelling of ginger, Mom stood in the doorway of my room. "I'm sorry, Izzie. I'm sorry he's gone."

"I really miss him," I said. "I try to pretend that I don't, but it's still there. All that pain."

Mom put her arms around me, and I could feel her breathing. "I know, Izzie. I know."

"What happened? Will you tell me now?" I said.

Mom pulled away from me and looked me in the eyes. "I tried to tell you as much of the truth as I thought you could handle at the time. You were only five. And you kept asking me if the serpent you had seen was real. I didn't want to frighten you, so I told you it was a dream."

I nodded. "And the flu?"

Mom shook her head. "You made that part up yourself."

"I guess it was easier than the truth."

"Yes." Mom took a deep breath. "We used to live in a place called Curvenal. Does that ring any bells for you?"

I thought for a long moment. "Not really," I said.

"A lot of people who had magic used to live there. It was a place for us to share our experiences. We still lived in the real world, but we didn't have to hide as much as we do here."

"Where is Curvenal?" I asked.

"North," said Mom. "In a valley between two mountain ranges. It's very remote, so we didn't get disturbed often by the outside, non-magical world. Your dad's family was from there, and it seemed like the perfect place to raise you. We knew from the moment you were born that you were special, that you had your dad's magic. You were hot with it."

I nodded, figuring I would ask her more about my magic later. Right then, I wanted to hear the story of my dad's death. It seemed like I had waited my whole life to hear the rest of it.

"We had rules about magic, and how it should be used. The rules were to help us protect each other and the outside world, the people without magic. It didn't seem right to use our magic to control other people, even though we could. And living together, we could watch each other to make sure none of us fell into that temptation. That was the idea behind Curvenal, anyway."

"But it didn't work?" I said.

She shook her head. "It worked for a few generations, but then a group of teenagers started looking into the ancient histories."

"What kind of ancient histories?"

"Histories of the old days, before there were rules about magic, before there was any power but magic in the world. The days of giant magical serpents."

"Real serpents," I whispered.

"They used some old spells and a map to search out the resting place of one of those serpents. Then they raised the serpent from its ancient slumber. Your dad could feel the change in his temperature immediately. He knew his magic was calling to something, and he followed its scent just in time to see the teenagers devoured by the serpent. For a few weeks, the serpent terrorized the town, devouring someone with magic each day, while your dad frantically tried to figure out how to fight it. Then it came for you and your magic, and he had to fight it.

"He left you in a cave where he thought you would be safe, but you were curious, and you peeked out. You saw it all, your dad fighting the serpent. And then him—"

"Dying," I finished for her.

She nodded. "The serpent called for you and tried to scent your magic, but you were too scared to use it. So the serpent slithered off, searching for you and for whatever other magic he could destroy. That's when I came and got you, and we left Curvenal right away."

"You left them?" I said. "With the serpent still there?"

Mom hesitated a long moment. "I couldn't fight it. Neither could you. You were a small child, Izzie."

"But all those other people . . ." I didn't like to think about how it must have been for the people who hadn't been able to escape from the serpent.

"Izzie, every time I drive someone to the hospital in my ambulance, every time I use a potion, there are others who are dying because I am not helping them. There are natural disasters all over the globe, and I can't be at all of them. Every day, I have to choose to save the person in front of me, the one that I can save. And that day, I chose to save you."

I felt as though a stone was being pressed on my chest; it was the weight of the responsibility that I had never known was mine. "You kept me safe all this time, and we could have been working against the thing that killed Dad?"

"When do you think I should have taken you back, Izzie? The year after he died, when you were six? When you were eight? When you were ten? I watched you, and I watched how little you showed an interest in your own magic. You were afraid, in some deep part of yourself, and you were right to be afraid."

"I'm still afraid, Mom. But I don't think I can let that stop me anymore. You've got to show me how to use my magic now." All I knew was that my magic made me hot, but that didn't seem particularly useful as a weapon against a serpent.

"That's the problem, Izzie. You have your dad's magic, and I can't really show you how to use it."

"But you had me spit in Tristan's potion," I pointed out.

"Yes. Your dad used to infuse my potions with one of the elemental powers."

"But what does that mean?"

"The elemental magic uses air, earth, water, and fire," said Mom, nodding. "It's very effective with certain potions."

"Then let's do it."

"Izzie, I don't know if that's a good idea."

"Why not?"

She threw up her hands. "It will draw magical creatures to you who are far more powerful than the slurg. The serpent has been sending them out after you for years, but they haven't been able to find you. Now they will try to taste your magic and kill you."

"Mom, I've already used my magic," I pointed out. "They're already coming after me. I might as well figure out something useful to do with it."

She sighed. "Come downstairs, then. That invincibility potion I've been working on could use some elemental magic added to it."

So I went downstairs, and Mom handed me a clear bottle with a pinkish liquid inside. When I opened it, the liquid smelled familiar, faintly sweet and herbal.

"I need you to enhance it."

"Tell me how to do it," I said.

"Well, your dad always said he just thought hard at something, and his magic came out."

"He thought at it?" I asked, skeptical.

"That's what he said."

"And what happened when he thought at it?"

"Well, there would be a wind, and then a wisp of smoke, and then the smell of clean earth," said Mom.

So I tried. I sat and held the potion in my hands. I thought at it for over an hour, and nothing happened. No hint of smoke.

"Maybe you should take a break," said Mom. "Come back to it later, after dinner."

But I was persistent. I ate a little dinner, but I have to say, the smell of the potion sort of killed my appetite.

It wasn't until I had almost fallen asleep in the kitchen and had started to dream of Tristan that I felt a sudden breeze. I looked up to see if Mom had opened a window, but she hadn't. And there was a trail of smoke coming from the bottle.

"I think it worked!" I called out hoarsely.

Mom came running from her bedroom. She looked at the bottle and at me and then sagged forward, her eyes closed. "It worked," she said. "Just like it always did when your dad was alive."

I held up the bottle and rubbed some of the liquid on my arm. Then I reached for a kitchen knife. Before Mom could stop me, I stabbed myself right in the arm. The knife glanced off and flew out of my hand, then fell onto the kitchen floor behind me.

"Cool," I said. Although that was just against a regular, non-magical knife.

Mom handed me the bottle.

I held it tight to my chest.

"I'll start making more," she said.

I held up the bottle and shook it. There was about a pint in there. How many days would that last? Three? Four?

I hoped Mom would work fast, because I didn't want to face something worse than a slurg without this.

Chapter 15

When the doorbell rang after dinner that night, I was surprised to see it was Tristan. He wasn't supposed to be out of the hospital until tomorrow, but he looked good, better than ever. His eyes were bluer, his smile brighter, and he looked great in his jeans and flannel shirt. I caught a glimpse of thick bandages around his chest under his shirt.

"Uh, hi," I said. Not the wittiest thing ever, but it was all I could do not to get all hot and sweaty around him again. I needed to keep my head on straight. The love philtre could make me feel in love with Tristan, but did I have to act on those feelings? Maybe I could stay with Mark after all. That was surely the more sensible thing to do. He was the one I knew and trusted. I had only just met Tristan, and even if he had saved my life, I didn't know anything about him.

"Can I come in?" he asked.

"Of course," I said, embarrassed that he'd had to ask.

He came in and sat down on the couch, his eyes on me the whole time.

I was suddenly conscious of how messy I looked. I had splatters of invincibility potion on my shirt, and I probably stank of vinegar. My hair was falling out of its barrette, and I was barefoot. Something about Tristan's being here made me wish I had on shoes and a nice jacket, as a kind of physical barrier between his body and mine.

"When did you get out of the hospital?" I asked, curling my feet against each other.

"Just now." He glanced down at my feet and then at my face.

Did he feel the same urge to touch me that I felt for him? He certainly looked calmer than I felt, but I tried my best. "You came here instead of going home? What about your uncle? Isn't he waiting for you?"

Tristan held up his hands. "Please, give me a moment. I will tell you everything I know." He took a deep breath. "But if you will not let me show my love, I must use some effort to contain it."

I felt like an idiot then.

"Who is it?" asked Mom, behind me. Before I could answer, she came in. "Tristan. I saw you at the hospital, but I don't think we've ever been properly introduced. I'm Izzie's mother, Gwen."

"Gwen," said Tristan with a nod. "I am pleased to meet you."

"Izzie has told me so much about you," said Mom.

"I wish I could say the same about you," said Tristan. "She won't talk to me much at all." He winced, then closed his eyes and took a few labored breaths.

He looked like he should still be in the hospital. "Can I get you something?" I glanced at Mom. Like the invincibility potion, for example?

Mom shook her head. "It doesn't work on past wounds. It's only a preventative, not a palliative. It's like a polio shot—no use after you've already got polio."

"How did you get here?" I said, looking out the window. I saw no car parked outside. Had his uncle dropped him off?

"I walked," he said.

"From the hospital?" said Mom. "That's ridiculous."

Knowing Tristan the way I did now, I didn't doubt it for a moment.

"That's over ten miles," said Mom when Tristan said nothing. "And you're injured. You shouldn't have—"

"I need to rebuild my strength," said Tristan. "I must be ready when an attack comes again. For Isolde's sake. And for the others."

"What others?" asked Mom.

"You know them," said Tristan, looking hard into Mom's eyes.

"Mom?" I said.

She sat down abruptly across from Tristan. "Curvenal," she said.

"You said you were from Parmenie. You said your parents died in a car accident, and you lived with your uncle." I stared at him, wondering what he'd told me that wasn't a lie. I guess a love philtre didn't make someone tell the truth.

Tristan looked away. I thought that would be a relief, but it wasn't. I felt sick and empty inside.

"My name is not Tristan, and I'm not from Parmenie," he said in a strange, low voice. He had always seemed optimistic and confident before. Now he sounded beaten. "Though the part about my parents dying is true.

I wanted to put my arms around him. But I also needed to hear the truth, so I waited for him to tell the rest.

He sighed. "They were killed, sacrificed to the evil Gurmun in order to save my life and the life of another innocent."

"I don't understand."

"Gurmun is the name of the serpent that killed your dad," said Mom.

I hadn't thought to ask Mom for its name. I didn't even know that magical serpents had names.

"Ever since he was roused from his slumber," said Tristan, "he has demanded a yearly sacrifice of one virgin male and one virgin female."

I blushed at the word, stared at Tristan, and blushed even more. "Why?" I finally managed to say.

"He was angry that he was put to sleep by magic centuries ago, and angrier still that your father tried to murder him after he had been woken."

I could feel myself becoming hot again, even though I tried to keep my magic from coming out like that. "I meant, why virgins?"

"Oh," said Tristan simply. "Because Gurmun believed the magic of virgins to be the most powerful in Curvenal. By killing them and taking their magic for himself, he would keep us all in slavery forever."

"And so far, it has worked," said Mom.

"For eleven years," said Tristan.

Eleven years, I thought. That was how long it had been since Dad died; that was how long I had been ignoring my magic and trying to live as if I was just a normal, non-magical girl in a normal, non-magical world.

"All this time, the sacrifices have been chosen by lots cast among the youngest and healthiest of the unmarried of Curvenal. And this year, the lot came to me. I was ready to die for my people." Tristan clenched a fist, and I couldn't help myself: I put a hand on his fist and felt the heat in my body dissipate.

"But my father would not let me," said Tristan. "He had raised me as a protector, for the one who would come to save us all from Gurmun. He took my place, he and my mother together, giving up their powerful magic to the serpent. They died so that I could come to you, Isolde, and bring you back with me."

He looked up at me and his eyes turned to slits. "I hated you when my father insisted that he would die in my place for your sake. I hated you when I had to say good-bye to my mother and leave her unprotected. Can you imagine what that moment was like for me?" asked Tristan.

I held tight to his hand, feeling my own strength increase. I didn't think that had anything to do with the love philtre, but I wasn't sure. "I didn't know that people were dying," I said softly. "I didn't know the serpent was real. I didn't even know about my own magic, Tristan. You have to believe me."

"I do believe you. Now that I have met you, I see the truth in your eyes. You are full of power and honor. That is what I meant when I said that we were the same, you and I. We belong to the world of magic. We must return to Curvenal and fulfill our destinies."

I dropped his hand. The idea of going back to the serpent was suddenly too much for me. I knew I should go. I had told Mom off for leaving Curvenal to the serpent. And now I was afraid. I had the invincibility potion, but it wouldn't be enough. It was one thing to protect myself against evil magical creatures. It was something else entirely to go out searching for them. Maybe I wasn't the person Tristan thought I was after all.

"But first," Tristan continued, "I must have my sword. I do not have the magic that you do, Isolde. But the sword holds the magic of my father, and his father, many generations back. It was forged a thousand years ago, and it has come to me at this time of urgency."

I was so busy watching his lips and listening to the music of his voice that I didn't realize he was asking for something until Mom responded.

"Of course. I'll get it," she said.

And then she left.

I shifted uncomfortably. "About this serpent in Curvenal . . . ," I said.

Tristan looked away, and his mouth, his kissable mouth, twisted. "You are afraid. That is understandable. But I will be at your side."

It turned out that something else the love philtre didn't give you was courage. And I kissed Tristan. I couldn't resist the need to feel his lips against mine, and I was pretty sure that after I said what I had to say, I wouldn't get the opportunity again.

We broke apart, breathing hard.

Then Tristan put his hand around my head and pulled me close again. He didn't kiss me. He just held me, running a hand down my face and neck and then up again.

It felt wonderful and terrible at the same time. I wanted more.

"Gurmun must die," he said roughly.

I shivered. I didn't know how to use magic except to make myself sweat and enhance my mom's potions. I could not defeat a serpent that had killed my father. I didn't think I could kill a garden snake right now.

Mom came back in and handed Tristan his sword. Tristan pulled it from its scabbard, and it seemed to sing as it caught the light in the living room. It was as tall as he was, and I could not see how he had hidden it at the football game.

Then he slid it behind his back, and it disappeared.

In that moment, he was amazingly handsome and powerful and brave. I loved him so much—almost enough to go with him. But not quite.

I swallowed hard and stepped away from him, looking to Mom for help.

"You said your name wasn't Tristan," Mom said.

How had I forgotten that part?

He shook his head. "It's Tantris," he said quietly, as though it was a big secret. "Tantris," he said again, with very precise pronunciation. His eyes were bright, and they bored into mine.

I nodded. Why was he making such a big deal out of that?

Mom went very still. "The son of Rivalin?" she asked.

Tristan—Tantris, whoever he was—nodded.

"And he is dead now?" she whispered.

"One week today," said Tristan. "As soon as he died, I came searching for you. The sword led me." Mom turned to me, looking very sad.

"Who was this Rivalin?" I asked impatiently.

"Your dad's best friend," she said. "You and Tristan used to play together when you were children."

I had no memory of that. I shook my head. It felt like everyone was trying to pressure me into doing more, being more than I was right now. It wasn't my fault that I was unprepared. Dad hadn't been here to teach me, and Mom had purposely kept me in the dark. Then Tristan had done the same, pretending to be an ordinary boy who was in love with me when really he had come to take me back to Curvenal with him. "You are a liar," I said to Tristan—or whoever he was—and I slapped his face. The stupid thing was that even as I felt the sting of contact, I wanted to throw myself at him. I didn't want to think about anything but us being together, no matter what the cost.

"Isolde, forgive me," said Tristan, and his voice was so humble that a part of me wanted to do just as he asked.

The part of me that wasn't thinking straight.

No wonder I had fallen in love with Mark. Mark, who was part of the regular world, who had nothing to do with magic. Mark was absolutely truthful. He was just what he seemed to be: the basketball captain at Tintagel High. I would never be surprised by him. That was the life I wanted: one of calm and certainty. Not this life, with Tristan and magic and serpents.

I was going back to Mark if he would have me. I wasn't going to let Branna have him—not when he was everything I needed.

"Just go," I said to Tristan. "Just leave me alone. And don't tell Mark anything. I think you owe me that much."

Tristan reached for my hand, and I jerked it away from him. I was not going to be fooled by my feelings again. They were from the love philtre. They weren't real.

Mom intervened. "Izzie, you may be upset with him, but I'm not going to send Tristan away like this. Were you planning on just walking home?" she asked him.

"Home?" he said distantly. "To Curvenal?"

"No. To your home here. With your uncle?"

He shook his head.

"Another lie?" I asked.

"Surely such a small lie cannot matter. When it comes to matters of import, I have always told the truth. I love you, Isolde. And I believe in you." Tristan's voice grew sharp on those last words.

"Believing in a lie does not make it true," I said.

Ever practical, Mom said, "But where have you been living? You must have somewhere to stay."

Tristan shrugged. "I have been sleeping here and there, under stairways, in alleys, or in underpasses. Or not sleeping at all. Even when I am lying with my eyes closed, I see things in my mind, real or imagined, that are too terrible to sleep through. I see a future in which Gurmun devours all those in Curvenal with magic, and he is still not sated. He will come for those in the unmagical world next. He will kill, and kill, and gain no magic. You cannot imagine the havoc he will wreak if he is left to satisfy his appetite for power."

"This is your new story to manipulate me into doing what you want?" I said scornfully.

"A story is not always a lie," said Tristan. "Some stories are truer than truth."

Truer than truth? That sounded like something liars made up to tell people who found them out.

"Are you going now? Or should I call Mark to make you leave?" Mark wouldn't do it himself, but his posse could handle the job while he watched.

"I will leave," said Tristan. He limped toward the door.

I wanted to go after him, but I didn't. That was magic driving me, and I didn't want magic anymore. "I don't want to see you at school," I warned him. "I'll tell them that you went back to Parmenie."

Tristan nodded. "Just . . . be careful," he said. "I could not bear it if something were to happen to you and I was not there to save you again."

Well, I was just going to have to learn to save myself, wasn't I?

Chapter 16

Mom tried to talk to me that night about Tristan, about Curvenal, about Dad, but I just shook my head and walked out of the room. I was finished listening to her, finished with her potions. I didn't even take the invincibility potion to school the next day. It was part of all the stuff I wanted to leave behind. I thought that if I locked down my magic hard enough and threw away the key, I'd be safe from Gurmun and everything else that was magical.

I wore Mark's varsity basketball sweatshirt, more as a statement to myself than anything. I didn't see Branna on the bus, and I wondered why she wasn't there.

When I got to school, I saw Mark in the pit and hurried toward him. It was only after I reached him that I noticed Branna there, along with Mel Melot. She was standing close to him—too close.

I had never gotten around to telling Mark to exile Mel. The day I'd meant to had been when Tristan first came and everything went crazy with the slurg.

"Izzie," said Branna, nodding to me.

"What's going on?" I asked.

Mel tilted his head to the side, and I watched in astonishment as Branna kissed him on the lips. "Oh, baby," said Mel, snuggling up to her.

I rolled my eyes and thought, *Seriously, do people still say that? Oh, baby?*

I was sure Branna would smack him or tell him how disgusting he was. After all, she was the one who had told me about him preying on freshman girls. And he had said he would get his revenge on both of us. But Branna didn't pull away from him.

"So, about Tristan . . . ," I started, trying to think about something other than Mel and Branna making out.

"I think he's still in the hospital," said Mark.

"No," said Branna, pulling her mouth away from Mel. "He got out."

"How do you know that?" I asked, surprised.

She glanced at me. "I checked on him. Just wanted to make sure that he was okay. Wasn't that what you wanted me to do, since you couldn't do it yourself?" she said. Was she trying to be best friends still?

If I hadn't been so mad at her, I would have felt sorry for her. Wasn't she the one who had said that she wouldn't try to manipulate someone into loving her, that she was going to wait for true love? I guess the waiting time was over.

"So did you see him?" I asked Branna. "Tristan?" Did she know that he was from magical Curvenal? Did she know that I had told him to get lost?

"No, I was just saying that I knew he got out of the hospital. Have *you* seen him?"

"No," I lied. If Tristan and my mom could do it, why not me?

"Well, he didn't come on the bus," said Rick Gawain. "So he must have decided to stay at home."

"Good," I said.

"What?" asked Mark.

"I mean, I think that was a wise choice for him. He almost died. He shouldn't try to come right back to school."

"Too bad," said Mark. "I was getting used to him being around."

"I'm sure he'll come back," said Branna. "He was getting used to being around, too. Wasn't he, Izzie?"

What was with her?

"I don't know," I said. "He was new here. Maybe he'll want to go back to his old school. With all this trauma, who could blame him?"

"But Parmenie?" said Mark with a laugh. "Come on. Tristan doesn't belong there. He belongs with us."

"You've never been to Parmenie, Mark," I said. "Maybe Tristan does belong there."

Mark's eyes opened wide, like I had never contradicted him before. Maybe I hadn't. I was still feeling confused about how I felt for him.

"I don't know. Tristan was pretty attached to you," said Branna.

"No," I said. "He wasn't."

"Gotta go," said Mel. He reached for Branna, and she gave him a kiss.

"What a lucky guy," said Mark as Mel moved off to class. Branna glanced at me with a flash of triumph in her eyes.

"Yeah," I said.

Mark leaned in to kiss me, too, but I turned my face to the side so his lips landed on my ear. Touching him still made me wince, but I told myself I was just going to have to get used to it. Tristan was not around anymore, and everything was going to go back to normal, even if I had to force it that way.

"I'm going to treat you like a queen now," he said. "I realize what I might have lost there."

"Yeah," I said. "Me, too."

"I have questions to ask you. About the future. About your past. So prepare for a long conversation."

That was not what I wanted. At all. But postponing it seemed like the best I could manage right now.

"Later," I said. I waved at him and then motioned to Branna. "I need a girl talk now. You don't mind, do you, Mark?"

Mark's face flushed as he looked at Branna. Bad sign, I thought. Bad, bad sign.

Then he turned back to me. "Sure," he said. "See you later."

As soon as he started to move away, I grabbed Branna's arm none too gently and pulled her over to the lockers on the west side of the commons.

"Don't try to tell me that Mel is the guy you've been pining after, Branna," I said in a low tone. "You're not in love with him, and you never have been."

"And you are the expert on love, I suppose," Branna said sarcastically. "Having been through it so many times in your life."

Arguing with Branna felt wrong. We had disagreed from time to time in the past, but we respected each other's opinions, and we'd never had catfights.

"So, are you going to be at lunch today?" she asked me, sounding cold.

"I think so. Why?" Why would I not be at lunch today?

"Just making sure," she said. "There might be something important going on then."

"What are you talking about?"

"Mel Melot," said Branna.

"Huh?"

"You know, I think I've figured Mel out, and he's not as bad as I thought. In fact, it turns out he's more open about what he does than certain other people I could name."

So now she was comparing me unfavorably to Mel Melot? When had I used my magic to make other people—well, except for that one time with the love potion. And then I had been trying to help.

"Fine. I'll be there if you want me to." I said.

She rolled her eyes.

"Hey, what does that mean?"

She said nothing.

"Branna, are you mad at me?"

"You think? How long did it take you to figure that out?" said Branna.

Ouch. "Okay, so is this about Mark? You want me to break up with him so you can have him, right?"

"He isn't right for you," she said.

"You mean because he's right for you?" There it was, out in the open.

Branna folded her arms across her chest. "Yes, he is. He's perfect for me. He's never been right for you. But you could never see it."

"How long has this been going on?"

"Does it matter?" Branna asked.

"It matters to me. I want to know how long you have been lying to me." Like everyone else.

"Fine. If you want to know the truth, I loved him before you ever hooked up with him. I loved him since we were freshmen. You didn't even notice who he was. I did."

"So you deserve him because you saw him first?" I asked.

"That's not what this is about."

"Then what? You could have said something before we got serious. I don't see how you can blame me." Surely, it was her fault as much as it was mine. She was the one who had kept her mouth shut instead of fighting for the guy she loved, even if I didn't think he would have picked her over me.

"Really? You went out with him once, and you were suddenly inseparable. I think you used the word 'boyfriend' before you even went out with him. What was I supposed to do? Make you pity me into breaking up with him?"

"No—I—Branna, I didn't know." I didn't pity her, did I?

Branna threw up her hands. "Of course you didn't know. You didn't want to know. And you could not imagine me having the audacity to fall in love with your boyfriend. You thought me so much below you that I could never even look up that high." She sounded fierce, and I knew that she had been angry at me for a long time.

"That isn't what it was like," I said.

"Then why did you never guess? If you knew me so well, if I was really your best friend, wouldn't you have been able to figure it out?"

It was a question I had no answer to. "I'm sorry, Branna."

"And so now you'll give him up to me?" she asked.

I still wasn't ready to do that. "Even if I did break up with him, that wouldn't mean he would fall in love with you." Mark wasn't a prize to give away. He was a person, with his own ideas, his own thoughts, his own feelings— for me.

Branna nodded. "I know that. But you could offer me some help."

"What, now you want magic?"

Branna shrugged.

I sighed. "Branna, magic isn't what it's cracked up to be. There are complications. Dangerous ones." I wished Branna had seen the slurg.

"Yeah. I knew you would make up an excuse."

"Really, Branna, if I told you what might happen if I used magic again . . ."

She stared at me. "You made Tristan fall in love with you. Even though you already had Mark. Didn't you?"

"It's not what it sounds like. I was trying to help you, Branna. I was."

She snorted. "Right."

"It was supposed to be for you. The love philtre."

"You were going to make me fall in love with Tristan so I wasn't in love with Mark? Thank you very much."

"No. I didn't know then. I didn't realize—Branna, I was trying to help, and then it all got messed up."

"Funny how it got messed up in a way that left you the center of the love triangle. Two hot guys fighting over you."

"They aren't fighting over me," I argued. I had always thought love triangles were lame. Girls who refused to choose between two good guys were the worst scum of the earth. And I didn't much like guys who let themselves be jerked around, either. But this was different.

"And me with no one," said Branna, "except Mel."

Well, now I understood why she was using Mel. She wanted to hurt me. She was going low enough that she couldn't avoid it. Only I wondered if she was going to end up hurt more.

She had every right to be mad at me. I could see now that I had been a lousy friend for a long time. It was amazing she had lasted this long without scratching my eyes out. But that didn't mean I was going to try another love philtre. I might not know much about magic, but I had learned something.

"I really don't think using magic or jealousy to get Mark is the right way," I said.

"Advice from one who has already seen love magic go bad?" she asked.

I winced.

"Then I won't ask you to do that. Just meet me in the cafeteria at lunch. I think I deserve that much."

Branna deserved more than that. But I wasn't about to give up my only hope of happiness, of a normal life, with Mark. Not even for Branna.

I told her I would meet her at lunch.

Chapter 17

Three hours later, Mel was kissing Branna at our regular lunch table. I sat with Mark while we tried to ignore them. Mark picked at his burrito supreme with Tater Tots on the side, both of them smothered in slimy-looking green salsa. The rest of the posse had finished and left.

Branna pulled away from Mel and stood up. She held a vial in one hand, and that hand was shaking.

"What would you say if I told you this was magic?" she asked, turning from me to Mark.

"Ha. Funny," said Mark.

"Izzie doesn't think it's funny, does she? Izzie believes in magic. Right, Izzie?"

"Uh, well . . . ," I said.

"Izzie's mom makes her own magic potions to help people in her ambulance. That's why Izzie insisted you call her mom's ambulance when she and Tristan were attacked by that dog."

"Seriously?" said Mark.

"It isn't like that," I said. Branna was outing me? I should have known that was why she wanted me in the lunchroom. But staying away wouldn't have helped, either, if Branna was determined. At least I could refute her, sort of.

"Then what is it like? Do you have some other explanation of why you wanted your mom's ambulance? She shouldn't have come for a relative, you know," said Branna.

"But my mom—" I didn't know how to finish without mentioning magic.

"Branna," said Mark. "This isn't funny."

"No, it isn't," said Branna. She motioned to Mel, and he rummaged in his backpack.

Mel looked around to make sure there weren't any lunchroom monitors looking our way, then pulled out another wine bottle, this one with different writing on it, but just as old-looking. He held it out to Branna.

"This is magic, too. Try it out," she said to Mark. "No matter how much you drink out of it, it will never go empty. Mel's parents don't know how to use magic themselves, but they have friends who do." She handed the bottle to Mark.

"And they are rich enough to buy whatever they want, even magic," she added, looking slyly at me.

I guessed that explained how they had gotten another ever-full wine bottle so quickly.

Mark lifted the bottle, and I thought, This is the end. This really is the end of us. "Looks like a regular bottle of wine," he said.

"It's not," said Mel smugly.

"So I'm supposed to drink this? Is this some kind of trick to get me in trouble?"

"I'll drink it if you like," said Mel.

"No, you won't," said Branna firmly. She nodded to Mark. "Go on, drink it. Drink as much as you can. You'll see."

Mark held up the bottle and took a sip. He made a face. "Cheap wine," he said.

"I never said the wine was good," said Mel.

Mark looked at me. "Do you believe in magic?" he asked.

When he said it straight out like that, I found I couldn't lie. "Mark—it's not what you think," I said.

Branna snorted. "Right. It's worse than you think. She's been hiding this from you all along, Mark. Lying to you."

Mark looked at me again, and I didn't know what to say. He raised the wine bottle again.

I shook my head. "Don't," I said.

But then he looked at Branna. And that said it all, didn't it? "Go on," she said.

So he drank. And drank some more. Then stared at the bottle and shook it. "Magic is real," he said in a hoarse whisper.

I stared at him. All this time, I'd been worrying about his reaction to my family's magic, but Mark was stronger than I had thought. He would have accepted it. He would have accepted all of me. But I hadn't really trusted him. I hadn't known him at all, just like I hadn't known Branna.

I looked at Branna.

She didn't look particularly triumphant, just determined. She held up the vial. "And this," she said, "is a truth serum. It only takes a drop, but for an hour afterward, whatever question is asked will be answered absolutely truthfully."

A truth serum? So Branna hadn't been using Mel just to make Mark jealous. She'd also wanted to get his magic.

"That would be interesting," said Mark.

"Wouldn't it?" said Branna.

Mark and Branna were looking at each other like I wasn't there. "What questions do you think you would ask," said Branna, "of me or of Izzie, if you could ask us anything you wanted?"

"I don't know," said Mark.

My only hope now was that the truth serum was a fake. It was a slim hope, though.

"Anything at all," Branna said slowly, exaggerating every word. Mark was watching intently.

"I dare you, Izzie," said Branna. And before I could say another word, she popped the cork off the vial. She put out her tongue and let one drop fall. The bottle didn't look like it had many drops left in it. I wondered who else Mel's family had used it on.

My eyes flickered to Mel. He had said he wanted revenge on us, and now he had it. What was more, he had Branna's help—and mine.

"Are you afraid of the truth, Izzie?" asked Branna. Her tone had changed, had become sort of sleepy.

"Are you?" added Mel.

"No," I said.

"Then why don't you take a drop?" asked Mel, coming closer. He took the vial out of Branna's hands and offered it to me.

Branna's arms were making a flying motion. Mel pushed her down, and she sat with a flop right next to Mark. She leaned toward him and nuzzled him.

"Hey," he said. "I'm Mark. Not Mel."

"I know who you are," murmured Branna.

"Your girlfriend is hiding something," said Mel to Mark. "Don't you want to know what it is?"

Mark hesitated, licked his lips, and glanced at me.

I took a deep breath. "Do you want me to do this?" I asked.

"I don't care. It's up to you. I don't tell you what to do," he said.

"But do you want to know the truth?"

Mark hesitated for a long moment. Then he gritted his teeth. "I'm not afraid of it," he said. "Not now. Not ever."

So I opened my mouth and let Mel put a drop of truth serum on my tongue.

It tasted like grass and roses. Then I felt this terrible desire to sneeze, but I was too tired to let the sneeze go. I felt the itching-sneezing sensation fall down my throat and into my heart, where it jumped around a bit. It wasn't a pleasant sensation, but at least it didn't hurt. After the serum had settled into me, I felt like I was too heavy to move, and I could feel my body sag forward onto the table.

"Do you love Mark?" was the first question I heard. I honestly wasn't sure who was asking it. It might have been Mel. It might have been Mark.

"Yes," I said.

"Do you love Tristan?" was the next question. I'm pretty sure it was Mel.

"Yes," I said.

There was an argument then that I only partly remember. I think Mark said that I could mean anything. I could love him as a friend, or as a brother.

"Do you love Tristan as a brother?" Mel again.

"No," I said.

"Do you love him as a friend?"

"No. I hate him."

Now Mark was crowing, happy that he had proved his point. But Mel wasn't done.

"You love him and hate him?" asked Mel.

"Yes."

"You burn for him?" asked Mel.

"Yes," I whispered.

"And Mark? Do you burn for Mark?"

I shook my head. "Mark is cool. Safe," I said.

"What's wrong with that?" said Mark, cutting in on Mel's questioning.

More argument.

Then another question from Mel: "Would you die for love of Mark?"

"No. Don't think so," I said. It was getting harder and harder to talk, to get words out, but the truth serum made me want to push them out, like bubbles rising to the surface.

"And for Tristan? Would you die for him?"

"Don't want to," I said.

"But would you? If he needed you?"

"Yes." I slowly put a hand over my mouth, as if to hold the word back. But it was too late.

I thought I heard Mel congratulating himself. Mark said nothing.

I couldn't move, couldn't speak. I could only listen to the rest of the interrogation.

"And now Branna," said Mel.

Had Branna planned it this way, or was Mel just taking it

to the logical conclusion? Either way, I could not deny that she was gutsy. Talk about putting yourself on the line.

"Branna, do you love Mark?" Mel asked.

"Yes," said Branna.

"Do you love Tristan?"

"No."

"Do you love me, Mel?"

Branna giggled, a stupid grin on her face. "No." She shook her head slowly.

Mel didn't seem too disappointed. I guess he knew what was going on and had just enjoyed himself while it lasted. "Do you love Rick or Will?" he asked next.

"No." Branna sighed and lolled back against Mark. He was staring at her, but he wasn't pushing her away.

"Do you love Izzie?" asked Mel.

"Sometimes. Sometimes I hate her," said Branna.

"And why is that?"

"She has Mark. She has him and I don't, and he doesn't see me. Most of the time. Although I think he might now."

"Would you die for Mark?" asked Mel.

"In a second," said Branna. "When can I? Where? How?" She lifted her head and looked around, her eyes bright even in her stupor.

"And do you care what Mark feels about you?"

"I care," said Branna. "Can't make him love me. Know that. But I can try. Have to try. Can't give up. Even if humiliating."

I could feel tears on my face for Branna.

"The truth serum is not a fake, Mark. You have to know that," said Mel.

"You knew she was in love with me? And you were kissing her like that anyway? What kind of a guy are you?" That was Mark.

I think he shoved Mel, but Mel didn't fight back. "Hey, I don't have a girlfriend," he said. "And she didn't have a boyfriend, either. So there was nothing morally wrong with me kissing her."

Were they going to beat each other up? I didn't care. The whole world felt distant and untouchable.

"There is when you know she's in love with someone else," said Mark.

"You weren't doing anything about it. She asked me to help her and I did. What's wrong with that?"

I heard more pushing and then a shattering sound.

"Do you have any idea what that's worth?" Mel shouted.

"Do you have any idea what a jerk you are?"

So Mark finally knew the truth about Mel. Mel would be exiled, but he probably didn't care about that. He had what he wanted.

"She asked me to help her get your attention. It's not my fault that she had to work so hard for it," Mel sneered.

"You took advantage of her," said Mark. "She was hurting, and you were enjoying it. In my book, that makes you a slimeball. Get out of here!"

Mel put up his hands and backed away. "Fine. That doesn't change the truth."

Mark looked at me and Branna.

I giggled. I felt very relaxed, an inch away from sleep.

"What am I going to do with you two?" said Mark. "I can't take you to the nurse. She'll think you're on drugs."

I couldn't find it in my heart to care about that. "Didn't mean to hurt you, Mark," I said.

"I know." He kissed me on my forehead. It felt just the same as before.

But then he looked at Branna. "Do you burn for me?" he asked.

"A volcano," said Branna sleepily.

Mark looked back and forth between us. "Now I know the truth," he said. "And I have to decide what to do about it."

"Magic," I whispered. "Real magic."

"That, too," said Mark.

And I fell asleep.

Chapter 18

When I woke up, I was still in the cafeteria, my face plastered to the table with drool. Not the most flattering pose to be caught in by your boyfriend. But after living through the humiliation of Mel's truth serum, it didn't seem to matter much.

"Hi," I said, sitting up and rubbing my face.

"Hi." Mark looked almost as bad as I felt, his face drawn and his eyes bright with strain.

What do you say to the boyfriend you just admitted you didn't burn for, when your best friend did? It was awkward.

"Where's Branna?"

Mark pointed to her. She was down at the end of the table, snoring.

I looked around the cafeteria. The food area had been closed up, and the tables and floor had been cleaned. I glanced up at the clock. "How did you get them to let us stay in here?" We were almost an hour late for class. Not that I really cared at the moment.

"I told them you two had been throwing up and you probably both had food poisoning," said Mark. "And if they wanted to make sure the school didn't get sued, they should leave you alone to recover."

"You didn't." Mark, the guy I thought was steady and normal? The one who would never lie?

"I did," he said with a hint of a smile.

I was starting to like him even more than I had before. Not that it changed the way I felt about Tristan. The love philtre was too strong.

"You didn't think I had enough imagination to pull that off, did you?" said Mark.

I shrugged.

"Nice to know that we can still surprise each other after all this time." Mark's voice was flat, and I knew it was over between us. I should have broken up with him days ago. I kept telling myself that I could reverse the love philtre, but I shouldn't have made Mark wait. I should have let him go free. To Branna.

And then there were all the things I had done wrong with her. My best friend, and I hadn't guessed the truth about her feelings? She was right: there was something selfish in my blindness. I kept holding on to Mark because he was familiar, instead of going for Tristan, who was dazzling and dangerous—and my destiny.

I was still scared about that.

"I'm going to be really happy for you two," I said. "In a few days. I swear." My voice was shaky, but I wanted to try to redeem myself in his eyes.

Whatever Branna had done to me today, I had done worse to her over the past year.

"Yeah, well, I'm not sure that's going to work as well for me with you and Tristan. You've only known him a few days. How can you know—already?" Mark asked.

In the end, it didn't matter that it was because of a love philtre. My feelings were what they were, and there was no getting away from them. I wasn't going to excuse myself with magic.

"You are a great guy," I said.

"That's what girls always say when they're about to break up with someone," said Mark.

I made a face. "Like you've had that happen to you so often."

"I've heard guys tell me about it plenty."

That I believed.

"Should I call him or something?" asked Mark. "Tell him you're his. Or he's yours?"

"Um. I have to talk to him myself, I guess." I didn't know what I was going to say to Tristan. The last time I'd seen him, I'd slapped him and told him he was a liar. I'd made him leave my house, even though he'd just been discharged from the hospital and had nowhere to go. The love philtre had made me love him, but apparently, it didn't make me treat him very well.

"You do that."

"You're okay with it? Just like that?" I asked.

"Okay with you breaking up with me? Okay with Tristan

stealing my girlfriend? I'm not okay with it, Izzie, but there's nothing I can do about it, is there?"

I looked into his eyes. I loved his dark eyes. But I loved Tristan more. "No," I said. "No more than I can do anything about you and Branna."

Mark looked at her, and I could see the way he tensed, ready to go to her if she woke up. Yeah, it was over between us, on both sides.

"We're still friends, right?" Mark asked gently.

"Of course. Good friends," I said. Even if I was an idiot who hadn't seen the truth.

"You and Branna won't hate each other after this, will you?"

"Well, I can't speak for Branna, but I don't hate her."

Mark sighed. "It's not like she's been trying to break us up all this time."

"No. She waited until she couldn't wait anymore. She was trying to be loyal, I guess." For over a year.

"When do you think she'll wake up?" asked Mark.

I checked my watch. It had been over an hour since lunch ended. "I don't know. Did she take more than the one drop I saw?" I stood up a little dizzily and went over to shake her shoulder.

She opened her eyes, but they seemed glassy. "You," she said, and then her speech went slurry and I didn't catch the rest. She fell asleep again.

I shook her again. "Branna, wake up. Come on."

She mumbled something.

I looked at Mark. "Can you come over here and help me?"

"I don't know anything about magic," he said. "What am I supposed to do? I don't want to hurt her."

He had been through a lot in the last day. Not only had he found out in the worst possible way that his girlfriend was in love with someone else, but he had found out that Branna loved him, and that magic was real, all at once.

"Come and kiss her," I said. Hey, it worked in the fairy tales.

Mark blushed.

I realized that Branna probably wasn't the only one who had hidden feelings for the past few months. All this time, I had thought he was just being nice, letting her come with us everywhere. And maybe that was what Mark had thought he was doing, too, at first. When it had changed, I could only guess.

If you knew exactly who you were going to fall in love with before it happened, then everything would be a lot easier. But you didn't get to plan things like that beforehand. You just had to scramble and figure things out once they happened.

"Come on, don't be shy," I said, beckoning Mark.

He came close to me, and I didn't think about how good he smelled or how my knees felt weak when he was around. I had never felt like that about him. I'd liked kissing him. I'd liked being next to him. But it had been nothing like with Tristan.

"I don't know. What if she doesn't want me to kiss her? It's not like we've ever talked about this. And I wouldn't want to be accused of—"

"Mark, she said she burned for you. I think we can safely assume that a kiss from you would be welcome."

"She seems drunk. You're not supposed to kiss a girl if she's drunk and not in her full senses," said Mark.

"You're kissing her to help her come back to her full

senses. Just a light kiss, nothing sexy about it. Pretend you're kissing your mom."

"On the cheek?" said Mark.

I sighed. "Like kissing a friend, then. On the lips."

Mark came closer. All elbows and knees, he seemed a lot taller and clumsier now than he'd ever seemed on the basketball court or in school.

Despite her size, Branna looked vulnerable.

Mark kissed her briefly and then I could see her start to kiss him back, even with her eyes closed. "M-Mark," she said softly.

Then she opened her eyes, pulled away from Mark, and gave a little shriek.

Mark put his hands up. "Hey, it wasn't my idea. Izzie made me do it. I swear, I wasn't going to touch you."

Branna's face fell.

Mark, you idiot, I thought. That was not what she wanted to hear.

"Well, thanks but no, thanks," Branna said to me.

At least she was awake now. She stood up, smoothed her hair off her cheek, and looked around. "Where is everyone?"

"Back in class," I said, "which is probably where we should be. Except I think you and Mark have some things to work out. Mark, why don't you go first?"

"Um, uh." Mark ducked his head like he was nine years old and giving valentines to girls in third grade.

"You have no right to tell him what to do, Izzie," said Branna. "I think he can make his own decision, and if he still chooses you, well, then, no one can say he did it blindly. You are the pretty one. Even if—" She stopped herself.

"You're beautiful, Branna," said Mark in a hushed tone. "I don't know why you never see yourself that way. I know I do."

"Oh? And when did this happen?" She sounded angry, but her eyes were glittering.

"I always knew you were beautiful. I just thought you weren't interested."

"You were dating my best friend," said Branna. Her voice was softer now.

"Yeah, she's easier to talk to. She doesn't scare me," Mark admitted.

Branna scared Mark? Oh! Just like Tristan scared me.

"Look, are you two going to throw everything away, or are you going to get it together?" I asked. I might as well have asked the same thing about me and Tristan. I wished he was here right then. But I was just going to have to go and get him, bring him back, and admit the truth about how I felt for him.

Branna blinked up at Mark. He leaned closer to her. She stood a little taller. He leaned in a little more.

It was just like that, a half inch at a time. Then they kissed again. For real this time.

My boyfriend and my best friend.

I clapped.

Branna looked at me, then ducked her head. "You must be really mad at me. About that truth serum. And Mel and everything," she said.

"I hate you," I said firmly.

Mark put a protective arm around her.

"But I also love you," I added.

I might have had to explain more, but the whole cafeteria started to shake.

"Earthquake," said Mark. He pulled Branna under one of the tables against the wall. Then he noticed me still standing in the middle of the room.

And he came to get me.

After everything I'd done to him, he pulled me toward Branna.

He didn't tuck himself around me when we got to the wall, though. He put an arm up to shield me from any large falling pieces of plaster or wood. But the rest of his body was reserved for Branna, who really could have protected herself just fine.

She didn't object, however. In fact, she looked pretty pleased with the position of Mark's body around hers.

The cafeteria kept shaking, worse and worse.

"Hold on," said Mark. "It should be over soon. Earthquakes don't last long."

I tried to think about the last time we'd had an earthquake. But we had never had an earthquake. Tintagel was in the middle of the country, to the north, and if we worried about any natural disaster, it was tornadoes, not earthquakes.

I heard something outside—a booming like the rumbling of a train or construction equipment.

Or the roar of a very large, very magical creature.

I saw something pass by the window of the cafeteria. It looked like an arm with a hand the size of a huge wrecking ball. Then there was more shaking as the arm moved away.

"Uh, Mark, Branna," I said. "I think there's a problem."

"There's an earthquake!" said Branna. "Of course there's a problem."

I pointed at the window, where a giant face peered closer and closer to the glass. The eye was the size of a big-screen television set. The nose was like a dripping, warty yellow car. The mouth was as wide as a wave on the ocean, and it was shouting into the window: "Come out, come out, Magic. Come out and fight!"

Magic. The slurg had called me that. The slurg, who had been sent by Gurmun, the serpent, to find me.

All these years, Mom had tried to keep me from using my magic, to protect me from the serpent and his servants.

And now here was another one.

A giant one.

Chapter 19

The school shook again and then the giant moved away, out of sight from the window.

I was breathing heavily, thinking that this time Tristan was not here with his sword to save me.

"What is that thing?" asked Branna.

"I don't know," said Mark. "Did it say something about magic?"

"Is the earthquake over?" asked Branna. She rose to her feet. Mark kept an arm around her as he stood, too, just in case.

I had a bad feeling about this.

"Branna, Mark. I think that was a giant."

"A giant? Are you sure those are real?" said Mark.

"Well, what's your explanation?" I asked. Then I added sarcastically, "You think an earthquake has a face and speaks?"

But Mark didn't have a chance to answer, because a stone

the size of a school bus suddenly crashed through the roof of the cafeteria. It was like an explosion, so loud that my ears screamed with pain.

When I looked up again, the stone was in the middle of the cafeteria, about ten yards from where I stood. All I could think, staring at the thing, was *Good aim.*

There was debris everywhere and rising dust that made it hard to see the blue sky outside, even though the sun was shining bright enough to make me blink. At least four tables had been cracked in the middle, and the linoleum floor was ruined.

The principal was not going to like this. I wondered if someone would try to blame me and Mark and Branna. But how could any of us have thrown a rock that size? It would have taken a crane to lift it, let alone throw it.

The shaking started again. I could hear people in the school around us screaming and running outside. Not a good plan, since the giant was out there. But staying inside didn't seem like a great plan, either. I didn't *have* a great plan.

"We have to get out there," I said. I couldn't let hundreds of helpless high-school students face an angry giant—not when he had come after me and my magic.

"You think we can get away from it?" asked Mark.

"No," I said, looking him in the eye. "I don't think I can. And I don't want to."

If the giant started going around the rest of the town to find me, that would just mean more buildings destroyed, more people hurt. And it would be my fault. If only I had taken my mom's invincibility potion when I'd had the chance . . . But I couldn't think about that.

We scrambled out through the cafeteria door. The frame was bent from the roof cave-in, but Mark managed to kick it out enough that we could squeeze through, though Mark and Branna had to pull and push each other. It was easier for me, because I was so small.

"Please tell me you've got your own magic," said Mark, looking out the big front doors of the school, toward the flagpole. Luckily, it seemed everyone else had run out the back door. I couldn't see anyone out front.

"I'm supposed to," I said, a little distracted.

I wondered when the police would be arriving, and what they would do when they saw a giant, which couldn't possibly exist. How much work was this going to create for my mother, who would have to erase the traces of magic? Was that even possible? Was there such a thing as an amnesia potion, and could she use it on everyone in town? Or did keeping magic a secret even matter anymore? After all, the secrecy had been to keep everyone safe from creatures like this giant. Now none of us was safe.

"So, what is your magic, anyway?" asked Mark.

"Elemental," I muttered.

"So that's, what, with the periodic table or something?" asked Mark.

"No. Not those elements. Earth, fire, water, air—the four elements," I said.

"Oh, good," said Mark.

Sure I had elemental magic, but I had no idea how to use it against a giant or anything else. I took a breath, straightened my shoulders, and stepped forward. I guessed it was time to learn.

"I don't think it's a good idea for you to go out there," said Mark.

"Well, I know it's not a good idea to go out there," I said. "But it's a worse idea to stay in here."

The giant was stomping around the parking lot, where the slurg had died. There were cars thrown everywhere like toys, except that when you throw toy cars, they don't break. They don't get pulverized by giant fists that look like they're crushing soda-pop cans.

The asphalt in the parking lot was getting ripped up, too. The giant was so heavy that his enormous feet broke through the surface. He bent over and yanked pieces of asphalt out and threw them or kicked them around. He seemed pretty mad that I hadn't gone outside yet.

I looked up the street, and I could see a couple of cars that had stopped where they were, without pulling over. Their drivers had gotten out and were fleeing in the other direction.

"I'll go," said Mark. "I'll fight it."

Before I could argue, Branna was suddenly wrapped around his chest. "No!" she said. "It will kill you."

She was right. Mark didn't have magic. Sending him out there was the same as handing down a death sentence, and even if I had been mad at him and Branna, no one deserved that.

"I can't just let Izzie go out there and face it alone," said Mark.

We watched the giant, which was the ugliest thing I had ever seen. I always thought giants would look like regular humans, just bigger. You know, twenty feet tall or something.

But this giant was nothing like a human. His head was

about half as big as the rest of his body, which should have made him unbalanced but instead made him able to pick up things and chew them. Like the oak that had been planted the year the school opened, forty years ago. We'd had a boring assembly about it in September celebrating the anniversary. It had been a big deal, and the house-and-garden store had planted forty saplings around the school for free.

Those saplings were nowhere to be seen. There was nothing green left outside. The giant was chomping everything in sight. He spat plenty, too. Like a wood chipper or a kid with watermelon seeds in his mouth. The missiles came through the front window of the school.

"The pit!" I shouted.

We all jumped into it, and it saved our lives. The stinky, smelly pit! I wanted to kiss the whorled black-and-gray carpet, but I didn't. I was saving my kisses for Tristan. In case I ever saw him again.

The giant had yellowish skin, and his eyes were dark purple with red centers that glowed like the eyes of demons in a stupid horror show. He had claws on the ends of his toes and fingers, and spikes growing out of his neck and all the way down his arms and legs. He was also naked, which was why I could tell that he was a he and not a she.

Let me tell you, a naked male giant is not pretty.

"Izzie, if you have magic, now is the time to use it," said Branna.

"I know." But how?

I could hear sirens in the distance now, coming closer. But I didn't see any ambulances or police cars yet. I hoped they were on their way.

"Try something. Something small," she said.

I don't know how long it would have taken for me and Branna to trust each other again in ordinary circumstances, though I think it would have happened eventually, because deep down, we were still friends. But the giant emergency sped things along.

"Like what?" I said.

"I don't know," said Branna, scowling at me. "You're the one who's lived with magic all her life. You figure it out."

So maybe the giant hadn't fixed everything between us.

"What about me?" said Mark. "You could turn me into a giant, and I could go fight the other giant."

"I don't think I can do that," I said. But how did I know, really? Mom hadn't explained anything about my magic, except about spitting in her potions and that it was based on fire, water, air, and earth. But how to use those against a giant?

"Try something," said Mark. "Anything."

So I did. I remembered when Mom had asked me to think about Tristan's healing potion in the ambulance. She said I should think about him getting better. So I thought about Mark fighting the giant. I thought about the giant falling over and starting to burn. I thought about it so hard I could hear my ears pop.

Then I looked at Mark and realized that his hands were on fire. The popping sound had been the skin on his palms opening up.

"Stop it! Stop your stupid magic!" said Branna. "You're killing him?"

But I had no idea how to control my magic. I thought as hard as I could about water, and icebergs, and smoothies, and anything cold and wet that I had ever seen. I thought of ice-skating rinks, and falling snow, and hail, and mountain streams with ice-cold water in them.

"Good. That's enough," said Mark, shivering. He had turned blue in the face, and there was a big icicle hanging off his nose. The whole school seemed colder, in fact.

"You're stealing all the heat from him," said Branna. She pointed at me, and I realized I was so dry I could have started a forest fire, and there was a faint scent of burning around me.

I let go of the magic, fire and ice, and crumpled to the floor, my harsh breathing echoing in the huge, empty halls of the school.

I lay there, thinking about how I might have used magic a thousand times in my life without even knowing it. About the chances Mom took with me, sending me to a regular school every day, with hundreds of regular kids. How could she have done that? I was a walking time bomb.

And I still hadn't even really figured out how to do magic yet, hadn't figured out the extent of my powers. It was overwhelming. I felt as if I was flapping around like a chicken with its head cut off.

"It's okay," said Mark. "I'm okay now."

That was enough to make me shake myself back to sanity. I had to get control of myself and my magic. I had no time to freak out.

I looked up, and Mark seemed normal again. Or mostly normal. He wasn't dead. In fact, he was kissing Branna.

Mark looked . . . glowing. I remembered how Tristan had looked like that after he'd drunk the love philtre. I had thought it was a magical thing, but apparently not, because Branna hadn't done anything magical to make Mark fall in love with her.

I stood up and took a deep breath.

Now the giant outside could see me, and it seemed that the use of my magic had made him even angrier. He shook his fist at me. "You! Magic! Coward!" he shouted.

Then he threw another rock at the school.

This one landed right in front of me.

If it had landed even two inches closer, I would have been crushed.

Was the giant toying with me?

I thought for a moment about the serpent from what I had thought was my dream. I wished I knew more about the elemental magic my dad and I shared. I was fighting a giant, though, so the same tricks he had used with the serpent might not work. And besides, my father had died fighting the serpent.

Maybe the giant wasn't as strong as the serpent, but that didn't make me feel better. It only made me surer I never wanted to meet the serpent.

I saw a helicopter above us, and the giant turned toward it and grinned. I thought of how small the helicopter would be next to him, and hoped it wouldn't come closer. Even if the people in it had weapons, what good would a gun be against a giant?

"Mark. I have something I want you to do," I said urgently. "What is it?"

"I want you to go get Tristan. Find him. He should be close by." Tristan had said he would protect me. "Tell him about the giant. Send him to help me." His sword would be a useful thing to have here, though I had no idea if Tristan would come in time. Or if he would come at all.

"Where does he live? Do you know his uncle's address?" said Mark.

I didn't try to explain to him that there was no uncle or that Tristan hadn't come from Parmenie. "Go look for him around town, in underpasses and stuff. He's not at home right now."

"He ran away?" asked Mark.

"Yeah," I said. That was the easy way of explaining it.

"Okay. I'm gone. What are you going to do?"

"I'm going to hold off the giant as long as I can." I tried to be brave, but my voice wavered on the last word.

"Branna, come on," said Mark.

"No," she said.

"What? You can't stay here. You don't have magic."

I turned around. Branna's jaw was set. I had seen that look before. "I can help Izzie," she said.

"I'm not going if you don't go," said Mark. "I can't." He looked at me, beseeching.

"Branna—" I said.

"Don't. You wouldn't let Mark tell you what to do. Why should I let him tell me what to do? He should go get Tristan, but I'm going to stay with you."

"You could get killed," said Mark.

"So could Izzie."

"But—"

"I'm her best friend." That seemed to be the end of the discussion.

Mark took a breath. "Promise me you won't do anything stupid," he said softly.

"I don't want to die," said Branna. "I have every reason to live—now."

Mark nodded, then turned to me. "You won't do anything stupid, either, will you?"

"Promise me you'll bring Tristan back," I said, eyeing the helicopter as it came closer.

"Promise," said Mark.

"Then go."

Chapter 20

You spend a lot of time in a high school. You get attached to it, even if it is utilitarian and box-shaped. You get used to the bright blue and yellow walls that are supposed to keep you alert in class. You get used to the rows of gray lockers, with the number 151 that bulges out on the side from the time a football player couldn't get it open and kicked it.

And then a giant comes in and ruins everything.

I had good memories of this school. Mark and I kissed for the first time here during a dance in the pit. It would never be the same now. Even if they rebuilt it, it wouldn't be the same place. Not to us. The big clock that hung on the wall above the pit like the eye of the principal, warning us that we were late to class, was dangling by a single wire.

Mark ran out the side door as the helicopter closed in.

The giant turned away, and I thought that was a good thing for Mark.

I cringed as the giant cupped his hands to his mouth and blew at the helicopter. That was all it took. The helicopter twisted in the air, then was pushed back. I didn't see it crash, but it went down hard somewhere.

The sirens from the police cars and ambulances stopped then, too. I hoped that meant they were going to hold off until they figured out what to do next.

But then the giant turned back toward the school and put his head down to the ground, his nose twitching.

"What's he doing?" asked Branna.

"I don't know," I said.

The giant started to move again, in the direction Mark had run.

What? No. That wasn't supposed to happen.

I started jumping up and down, shouting at the giant, trying to get his attention.

But the giant looked like an enormous bloodhound, sniffing along.

"The elemental magic," said Branna in a hollow tone.

"Right. From when I almost set Mark on fire," I said, understanding. "The giant can smell my magic." And now the creature was following Mark.

"I'm going after him," said Branna.

She thought that would help? "No. I'll do something." What, I had no idea.

I could just see the hind end of the giant disappearing behind the edge of the school. I ran out the front door, though why I bothered with doors, I don't know. There were plenty of holes in the walls.

"Giant! Come back!" I shouted. "I'm your magic!"

But he didn't come back. Stupid giant. You'd think with a big head like that, he would have a few more IQ points.

"Giant!" I kept jumping up and down, screaming. I wasn't going to let the creature hurt Mark. Or Branna.

I could hear him sniffing around beside the school. Then I got mad. I didn't mean to focus my magic, but I guess I did it anyway. I felt a fireball shooting out of my hand in the giant's direction. It wasn't pleasant. It was terrifying, actually. But I was using my magic now.

Branna came running up beside me.

"Shhh!" I told her, and put an arm out to keep her from going any farther.

I heard the swish of the fireball, then a thunk, followed by a sizzle and a roar. Then I saw some smoke.

The giant turned back, trailing smoke, and started moving toward me and Branna.

"Branna, get out of here!" I called.

"Not until you come with me," she said.

Did I mention how stubborn Branna can be? And how she never does what I tell her to?

"Branna, I don't know if I can control my magic," I shouted. "I don't know if I can keep it away from you!"

She didn't listen.

"You're not facing this alone," said Branna.

I stared up at the giant, who looked pretty angry. Blood dripped from under his left eye, where the fireball had hit him. I think it was blood, though it was blackish red, not regular red like human blood. His giant mouth was twisted into a parabola. (Even at that moment, I felt smug that I'd learned that term in math.) His nose was dripping, and part of the reason I started to run was to get away from what-ever was coming out of his nostrils. It looked like thick glue, and whatever it touched slowly began to melt. I could see the evidence all around the school yard, where even cement blocks and shards of glass had melted.

"Magic!" shouted the giant in a low voice that was enough to make me feel like another earthquake had struck, right in my heart.

Aren't people who have magic and fight giants supposed to be brave? Well, I wasn't.

"Run, Branna!" I said. I tore back into the school through a broken window, Branna right behind me. We took shelter again in the pit. My arms were wrapped around my body as I rocked back and forth.

Branna must have been wondering how she had gotten stuck with a best friend like me, blind and stupid as I was.

"Magic?" said the giant. "Where Magic go?" He was clearly unhappy, and he expressed it in his eloquent giant way: by collapsing onto the plaza in front of the school and punching the cement patio.

The cement flew up and peppered the windows around us. It was worse than when he had thrown the giant boulders, because there was no way to avoid all the flying shards of cement. I got one in my cheek, and let me tell you, it hurt. Then one hit my knee, and another lower, on my calf.

Maybe you think that after you've been attacked by a giant, hit by a few chunks of cement, and almost killed by thrown boulders, you'd be too scared to feel pain. But that isn't the case.

Branna was even worse off than I was. She'd been hit in the head by one of the larger pieces, and her blond hair was turning red with her blood. "Now what?" she asked in a low voice.

She must have been wishing by then that she had left with Mark after all. Or that she had never met me.

"I'm going to try to use magic on your head," I said. "To heal it." If I'd had one of Mom's potions with me, it would have been easy. But even if Mom was in one of the ambulances up the street, she wouldn't arrive in time to help Branna.

I tried to put myself into a trance to focus, terrified that a fireball would come right out of my hands and sink into Branna's bleeding wound or that I would inadvertently turn her into a newt. Or that I would somehow call another giant and then we'd have two to battle.

There were probably a lot of wrong ways to use magic. But the only way I'd had success with it by myself was with fire. If only I could control it a little bit . . .

"You can do it, Izzie. I've always known that. You can do anything you want."

I felt fire in my hands, and I jerked away. "Branna!" I cried out.

But she wasn't on fire. She wasn't shrieking in pain. She put her hands to her head and felt along the top, where the worst wound had been. "It's healed," she said.

"Really?" I put my hand out to touch it. It wasn't sewn up neatly the way they do it in the hospital. It hadn't disappeared, either. It was sealed up as if it had been cauterized with a very small, precise iron. It was still a little hot to the touch.

"Does it hurt?" I asked. I felt the other spots that had been bleeding, and they were the same.

"A little. Not as much as before, though," said Branna.

"You should go now," I said. "Before it gets even worse."

"If I left now," said Branna slowly, "the giant would smell your magic on me. It would come after me like it went after Mark."

I hadn't thought of that. "Right. Bad idea. You stay here. I'll go out." I stood up.

Branna pulled me back. "No, I'll go out. Distract it. Make it think I'm you. Then you can attack it from behind. I bet the magic you did on me will make me smell even more like you than Mark did. Besides, I'm female, too. That might confuse it."

But Branna didn't look anything like me. Unless . . . I took off my sweatshirt and handed it to her. I loved how soft it was after Mark had worn it so much. I had always felt like he was next to me when I wore it, like he was telling me that I was his and he was mine. It seemed wrong for me to have it now, anyway.

It was a faded red, and it smelled of fire. Magical fire. That was one of the elements. But what about the other three? How could I use them to fight the giant? Earth and water and air.

"Thanks, Izzie," said Branna. She pressed her hands gently against the fabric of the sweatshirt and pulled it over her head. "Ready?" she asked.

"I'm ready if you are," I said.

She ran out to face the giant with her head held high, confident, powerful, like she believed she could kill it. Or I could. Maybe it was an act, but if so, then she is the best actress ever. If I was the giant, I would have run away, yelping in fear.

She held her hands out in front of her. "Giant," she said

in a strong, loud voice, without a hint of fear. "I am Magic. You wanted me?"

The giant straightened up to his full height. He had been hunched over, peering into the school through the windows and attacking small objects on the ground. Now he was ready for a real battle.

"Magic," he said with satisfaction. "You are not coward."

That didn't make me feel so good, because I was still inside the school, and did that make me a coward? I was being tricky; that was all. I was outsmarting the giant, like you're supposed to when you're fighting someone bigger and stupider than you. That's what happens in all the fairy tales, right?

"No. But I will give you one chance to flee before I burn you to a cinder," threatened Branna.

I started moving. I needed to be in a hidden location for this to work, a place where the giant wouldn't immediately see me and smash the roof in. I couldn't stay inside, as tempting as it was. Its safety was an illusion. The giant could come in anytime. He just wanted to make sure he was killing the "magic."

I went outside through a broken window, and I felt the glass cutting into my arms and neck, making me bleed. But I didn't dare use my magic on myself right now. I had to save it for the giant.

I saw a row of cars that had been thrown together in clumps. Grimacing in pain, I tucked myself behind the first one, ready to leap to the next one as soon as I had to.

"No chance," the giant said to Branna. "No run away. I kill you."

"That's not going to happen," said Branna.

The giant put down his hand and picked her up.

I winced at the sight of Branna being lifted sixty feet into the air, higher than a Ferris wheel. She still acted as if the giant could not hurt her. I don't know how she had the courage to stay so calm.

Branna was right next to the giant's face now, and he was examining her carefully. Maybe he was nearsighted. Who would make glasses in that size?

The giant opened his mouth.

I thought how bad his breath must smell from up close. It was bad enough where I was, yards away. I didn't think he was a vegetarian. He looked at Branna like she was a tasty treat, a bite-size chocolate-covered ice-cream bar. He wasn't going to worry about the calories, either. Guys never do. They want to be bigger.

"Let me remind you: you were *sent* to kill me. Isn't that so?" asked Branna.

"Does not matter," said the giant.

"Well, why didn't whoever sent you come himself? I'll tell you why. Because you're the first wave. I'm supposed to use up all my strength on you so I don't have as much for him. He doesn't think you're going to win, though. You're just collateral damage."

"Magic use too many words," said the giant. His nose twitched. I thought, *I've got to do it now. No more waiting.*

I concentrated on the image of a giant fireball, and I sent it right at the giant.

It wasn't as big as I had hoped. I was afraid of hitting Branna, but luckily, the fireball hit the giant in the shoulder.

He batted it down, and then his hand was on fire. It was the hand that held Branna. .

"You see? You are going to die, giant," said Branna, tucking herself away from the fire as much as she could.

Was he going to be fooled by her charade long enough for me to send another fireball? Were the police and the other rescuers going to stay away long enough to give me a clear field?

I hoped so.

This time, instead of trying to send out one big fireball, I sent out a shower of them, one after another. It didn't take as much strength that way, and the giant couldn't avoid them all. They peppered him, and at first he just hopped on one foot or made a face. But they kept hitting him.

He dropped Branna. "Not Magic," he said, and turned toward me.

I jumped to the next clump of cars as he reached down and threw the flagpole in my direction. Whether he had bad eyesight or not, he speared the place where I had been perfectly. It was unnerving, looking at the flagpole shivering in the ground exactly where I had crouched a moment before.

"Magic!" shouted the giant. "Come fight me. Coward!"

But I kept up the fireballs. Small and steady does the trick.

For a second, I stopped, because I couldn't see Branna, and I was afraid she was in the way. But then she limped around the giant, toward the doors to the music room on the north side of the building. So she was still alive, still moving.

I kept up the attack.

The giant kept throwing things in random directions,

desperate. Then finally, he fell down. The fireball that did him in went straight into his eye and must have bored into his head. I watched him for several seconds to make sure he didn't get back up, but I didn't touch him or check to see if he was still breathing. I figured he would try to attack again if he could. He hadn't seemed the type to fake dead and try to get away.

His body was still smoldering on the ground when I saw Mark and Tristan run forward, ducking down so they wouldn't be seen by any of the police cars.

Chapter 21

I looked toward where Branna had gone, but she wasn't visible above the rubble. I figured she must have gotten inside the school somehow. Mark was where I had last seen her, and I thought he would go inside, too.

There were wires hanging everywhere, from the streetlights the giant had taken out. Everything was a terrible mess. I wondered how we were going to avoid people's learning about magic once they saw the wreckage—not to mention the giant's body.

The school wasn't completely ruined, but I didn't think we'd be having classes there anytime soon. There was going to be a lot of cleanup: the debris, the broken roof and mangled walls, the windows. I hoped the school had a budget for this.

"Isolde!" cried Tristan. He ran to me, threw his arms around me, and hugged me so tightly I could hardly breathe.

I squawked, and he put me down. "Forgive me. I did not mean to hurt you. Are you all right? How did you defeat the giant?"

"I think I've figured out my magic," I said. "Or part of it, at least."

"Oh?"

I held out my hand and thought about Tristan. A fireball grew in my palm, and I kept it there, glowing red and yellow, while Tristan stared. "I can make these," I said.

"That is good news," he said cautiously.

"I shouldn't have yelled at you yesterday," I said. I had a lot to apologize for, and I knew it. Maybe now wasn't the best time, with all the destruction around us, but I didn't want to wait anymore.

"I did not tell you the full truth," Tristan admitted. "And it is true that I wanted you to come with me to fight Gurmun from the beginning."

And that was so selfish and deceitful of him? Ha!

"You must think I am so shallow," I said. "I don't know why you even stayed here for me, but I am glad you did." I put my hands to his face and felt his lips, his cheekbones, his eyebrows. Every part of him was delicious to touch.

"I stayed because I could not leave," he said. "I stayed because there was no place for me to go if you would not be mine. No house could be a home; no sunrise could be warm and light if you were gone from me. I need you. Without you, I do not think I could live." It was pretty dramatic stuff, but the way Tristan said it, I believed him.

"I feel the same way." I pulled him closer. I knew that people were going to be coming soon, police and everyone else. But Tristan and I had this moment to ourselves.

We kissed. It was a feeling I will never forget. His lips were soft, but he was cold. He had been outside in the elements for the past day and night. Feeling his arms wrap around me was like finding a coat that fit me perfectly, that had been made for me. He was the kind of guy I had never dared imagine could be mine. I didn't know someone like that could exist in any world, let alone in the one I was in.

I loved the way he tasted salty and sweet and sour all at once. Maybe the love philtre had pushed us together sooner, but I couldn't believe that it wouldn't have happened anyway. True love doesn't let anything stand in its way. It really does conquer all.

Suddenly, Tristan pulled away from me.

"What?" I reached for him.

"You killed her!" Mark shouted. "I left her with you. I trusted you. And you killed her. Branna and I hardly had a chance to know each other."

"Branna?" I said. I looked toward the north doors to the school, and I saw a heap of clothes I had thought was rubble. But how? The last time I had seen her, she had been standing up, hurt but alive.

"Yes, Branna. Did you forget her already? What did you do to her? I thought you were going to protect her!" I had never seen Mark like this before, even when the basketball team had lost the state championships last year because Will had missed a foul shot at the last buzzer. Mark had punched a hole in the locker room wall that night and broken his hand in three places, but that was it. Now he was shaking his fist at me.

"She—she wanted to help," I said haltingly.

Tristan quickly moved between us. "Leave Isolde be. She needs time to recover from the giant's attack. She has other things she must do with her magic now that she has discovered its true nature."

Mark yanked on Tristan's shoulder. "I don't care an ounce about her magic and what she can do with it. Her magic is what got Branna killed."

Tristan's mouth closed tightly, and I could see the line of his jaw grow taut.

"Mark, don't do this," I said. "Let me see if Branna is—"

Mark punched me in the face. Mark, the steadiest guy in the world. The guy who made me feel safe whenever I was with him. The guy I loved like a brother and a friend.

I was so stunned that I just gaped at him. I didn't even try to shield myself from a second blow.

He swung at me and he would have hit me again, except that Tristan caught his hand. There was a sound like flesh hitting wood. And it wasn't the wood that cracked.

Mark made a low grunting sound. Then he turned to Tristan. "If you want a fight," he said, "I'll give you a fight. You think you can touch me? A runner from Parmenie? What are you going to do, make me chase you to death?"

Mark was several inches taller than Tristan. And Mark, though he wasn't a weight lifter or anything, had muscles. Tristan wasn't without his own muscles, but they were more compact. It was like a semitrailer meeting a sports car: when they crash, everyone knows who is going to win.

"Stop it, you two!" I shouted.

They were circling each other, feeling out weaknesses.

"Keep out of this, you witch!" said Mark.

"Find yourself a safe place for a little while, until I am finished," said Tristan.

Like I was going to do that. I jumped up on Tristan's back and pounded on him. "Don't hurt Mark!" I said. Right then, Mark kicked Tristan in the stomach.

I slid off Tristan's back and yanked on Mark's arm. "If you really care about Branna, why are you doing this? You should be helping her." It had only been a few minutes since I saw her go down, and I knew this was the last chance we were going to have before the police came in and decided to do things their way.

"She's dead," said Mark.

"There's dead, and then there's dead," I said. Mom had taught me that was true even if you didn't have magic. There was a certain length of time before the heart couldn't be restarted. It depended on the temperature (colder was better), and also on how much exertion the person had been engaged in at the time of death (less was better). And also on magic. Mom had potions that could bring people back to life if they had died valiantly and were still supposed to be alive. She had explained it to me once, but I hadn't listened very carefully.

While I was distracting Mark, Tristan landed a fist in his face. Then he whirled around, caught Mark's leg with his, and pulled him down.

I fell down, too, right between the two of them. Now I was mad.

"You are not helping me!" I shouted at Tristan. I needed him to calm Mark down, not make him more upset. They got up and started circling each other, grimacing. I pushed between them.

But neither of them was listening to me. I was going to have to stop them—and fast. We couldn't stand around fighting while Branna was lying there, dead or close to it, and the police were about to come storming in any minute and put us all in custody.

I didn't even have to think about the magic. It just happened automatically. I felt the heat inside me, anger and frustration and sadness and fear coming together and bursting out of me. I threw the first fireball at Mark, right into his mouth, which was wide open.

He looked like he had swallowed something unintentionally and was about to throw it back up. Then he stepped back, arms wheeling, and let out a huge smoking belch. It hadn't been a big fireball, but he clutched his stomach and went down.

"Mark!" I shouted. I hadn't meant to hurt him; I was just trying to get him to listen.

Tristan ran toward Mark, and I thought he would kick Mark while he was down. So I threw a small fireball at Tristan, too, and it hit him in the back. I heard a sizzling sound, like when I had hit the giant with all those fireballs at once.

"Tristan!" I shouted as he fell forward onto Mark.

I rushed to him and rolled him off Mark. He smelled of smoke and magic. I kissed him on the lips and then on his eyes and his forehead and his cheeks and his chin. "Tristan, Tristan, Tristan."

Love makes you say stupid stuff, though I don't think it technically lowers your chances of a scholarship.

He breathed and folded his arms around me again.

But I couldn't waste another minute. I had to help Branna. Life and death before romance seemed like a good rule.

I hurried over to Mark, who had somehow gotten up and was kneeling by Branna's body.

"Don't touch her! You gave up the right to anything of hers!" Mark shouted at me.

I ignored him and bent over Branna. I could see now that there was a piece of wood sticking out of her back. It must have gone straight through her when she fell. Seeing it made me cringe. There was blood soaking into her clothes and onto the ground around her.

But blood pouring out meant she was still alive, didn't it?

I put my fingers to her throat to check for a pulse and couldn't find one. Was I just too nervous?

"Branna? Branna, talk to me."

Her mouth twitched.

She wasn't dead, then. But she would be soon unless I could figure out how to get her to Mom. I couldn't move her, because the wood was stuck in her, and I couldn't get the wood out, because that would just make her bleed faster.

"Mark!" I said. "Talk to Branna. She's alive. See if you can get her to respond to you." If she was fighting, that was half the battle. Mom had told me lots of stories of people who had come out of things that no one expected them to, mostly because they had people talking to them, reminding them of what they had to fight for, why they should live even if it hurt.

"We never had a chance," said Mark. "I had just found her, and now she's—"

"Quit it," I said sharply. "You're going to have all the time you need with her. Tell her all the things you're going to do when she's well again. Dances you're going to take her to. Cool places you'll go. Movies you'll see together." All the things I used to do with Mark. But I wasn't jealous at all. I had Tristan, and I really wanted Branna to be happy. And alive.

Minus the piece of wood in her chest.

Tristan sat down next to me. "What can I do?" he asked. "I have my sword, but it seems of little use now."

"Do you have any healing magic?" I asked. "Maybe a potion or something?"

Tristan shook his head. "My magic is of metals. That is why I have always used it through the sword."

"Metals." I'd never heard Mom talk about that.

Tristan shook his head. "It is called alchemy in some parts of the world."

He was an alchemist, my mother was a witch, and I was a sorceress. This was all too confusing. "Give me some space to think. I need to gather myself and my magic."

My power to cauterize had worked on the cuts on Branna's head. I couldn't do it before I took the piece of wood out of her, though. I had to take out the wood and then cauterize her wound immediately, to make sure she didn't bleed to death. I couldn't do that alone.

And it wouldn't fix everything. Some internal organs probably had been injured. I didn't dare to try to use my power on them. I wished I had already taken human anatomy, like Mom had told me I should, my sophomore year.

"Mark, do you have your cell phone?"

He looked up at me, startled. "What?"

"Your cell phone. Get it out. Call my mom. She'll tell me what to do." Maybe she was already here at the school with her ambulance.

Mark's fingers were shaking. He dialed wrong twice.

"Give it to Tristan," I said.

So Tristan took the phone, and he pressed each number deliberately, to make sure it went through. Then he handed the phone to me.

"Izzie? Is that you? Thank goodness!" said Mom.

I was so relieved to hear her I could feel tears pricking at my eyelids. "Where are you, Mom?" I asked her.

"I'm a block away from the school, in an ambulance. Where are you? You weren't with any of the kids who escaped the earthquake."

"Mom, it wasn't an earthquake," I said.

There was a pause. Mom said quietly, "I know that, Izzie."

"It was a giant."

"I know," she said again.

"It's dead now, but Branna is badly hurt. She's barely alive."

"Okay, listen, Izzie. Is there anything the police will see if they come in now?" she asked.

I glanced around, realizing what she meant. "The giant's body," I said.

"Is there any way to prevent that?"

From the way she was talking, I could tell that she was with someone else. She hadn't said a word about magic.

"I could burn it," I said. "With fireballs."

"You need to do that," said Mom.

"But Branna—" I argued.

"Do it," said Mom. "Now."

She had told me before how important it was that I didn't tell people about magic. She'd described the havoc it would cause if people everywhere started to search for it and use it without understanding. Or if they tried to call magical creatures, like this giant, thinking they could control them.

I had to trust my mom.

"Okay, I'll do it," I said. I started a fireball in my hand.

Mark's eyes went big, but he didn't say a word.

I threw fireballs at the giant's body again and again, until it was a smoldering mess that could have been anything.

"Done?" asked Mom. I had forgotten she was still on the line.

I was breathing heavily.

"Done," I said.

"Okay, now I can come in and help you. All right?"

"Please," I said, and as soon as I said the word, there was a rush of movement toward the school. I saw police with guns raised, though the giant was no threat now. Behind them were the rescue workers, and with them, Mom.

Chapter 22

Mom ran toward me, her emergency kit bouncing on her hip.

"Are you okay?" she asked. She pointed to my shoulder and arm. Looking down, I remembered I had cut myself on the broken window. I hadn't noticed any pain until now, but my wounds suddenly started to throb. Branna was the one who needed emergency help, though. I could wait.

"Branna!" I said urgently, and pulled Mom toward my best friend.

Mom knelt down by her still form. She lifted her head and felt for a pulse, then sighed.

"Do you have a potion for her?" I asked.

"A potion will have to come later," said Mom.

"She's going to wake up, right?" said Mark.

Mom didn't say anything about Mark's rather obvious change of allegiance. "I'll do everything I can, but I need your help." The other rescue workers were spreading out, checking through rubble and entering the school building. I didn't know how many people—if any—were left inside. I hoped that no one was seriously hurt—and that nobody had seen the giant close enough to realize it had to be magical.

"I need you to lift her up," Mom said to Mark. "Then you, Tristan, pull out the wood."

"Are you sure?" asked Mark. His lips were cracked and bleeding, and his whole face was pale. I wondered what kind of internal injuries he had from the fireball and everything else. But he was still standing and Branna wasn't, so it was Branna we focused on.

"Izzie, you need to use your magic to seal her organs. Once the wood is out, I will guide you through them one by one."

I took a deep breath. "Okay," I said, glad she was here to help.

"Ready?" asked Mom.

"Ready," Mark and Tristan said in chorus.

It gave me hope that they could actually work together when necessary.

"Ready," I said a second later. I wanted to close my eyes, but I forced them to stay open.

Mark lifted Branna.

That was when Mom saw how big the piece of wood was. It was stuck in the ground underneath Branna.

"She's bleeding," said Mark. "Hurry!"

"Tristan," said Mom. "The wood has to come out of the ground."

He bent under Branna, put his hands around the piece of wood, took a deep breath, and pulled. The wood stayed wedged in the ground where the giant must have thrown it when he tried to spear Branna with it.

"Tristan, do it!" said Mom. "This is your chance to prove yourself."

I thought that was totally unfair, but Tristan seemed to get energy from the challenge. He shook out his arms and stared at the piece of wood like it was an animal he was hunting. A mastodon or something really large. He bared his teeth, made a sound deep in his throat, and pulled again.

For a long moment, nothing happened. Then the wood started to slide.

Mark stumbled backward with Branna.

Tristan pulled the wood out of the ground and then out of Branna. Then he whirled it around like he was doing the shot put and sent it out toward the football field.

I'd seen Tristan against the slurg, but that was with the sword. This was superhuman strength. No wonder when Mark had seen him run, he'd been eager to make sure he was on Tintagel's track team.

"Izzie, come here," said Mom, beckoning me closer.

Mark was holding Branna against his shoulder. She was motionless.

"Here, and here," said Mom, pushing my hands into the right positions along Branna's back.

I put away my pain and focused on my magic, on the feeling of fire.

"Slowly," Mom warned me.

So I let it out slowly. It was the hardest thing I had ever done in my life—harder than killing the giant. That had been just one fireball after another, with no attempt at finesse.

This was like a chemistry experiment, but without using my hands, just my thoughts.

"And here and here," said Mom, nodding at each vertebra, the lungs, the heart, showing me where to seal.

Branna whimpered.

She would have a terrible scar, but I thought I was doing a better job than an emergency room doctor would. There were lines left where the wound came together, but there weren't any cross marks from stitches, and there were places where the wound was almost invisible. The lines were bright red and shiny, but they would fade. I hoped.

"Are you sure you're doing this right?" asked Mark.

"This is her only hope," said Mom. "Just talk to her, Mark. Keep her with us."

Mom turned Branna to the side and I gasped at the damage on her stomach. I wanted to close my eyes, but I couldn't. I had to keep them open and follow Mom's instructions to the letter, step by step, healing her on this side, as well. Spleen, stomach, intestines, liver, and all the rest.

"Mark!" Mom said harshly. "Talk to her."

So Mark did, his voice as intimate as if he and Branna were alone. "I'm going to take you to the Halloween dance, and you can dress up as an Amazon and I'll be your slave. Or we can do something romantic. Romeo and Juliet. Or Lancelot and Guinevere. Or Mr. Darcy and Elizabeth Bennet."

I was surprised Mark even knew all those love stories. I guess that was more about him I had never bothered to find out. I bet Branna knew them all, too. And I bet she knew that Mark knew them.

"Branna, just please come back to me." Mark spoke from

his heart, with no hint of embarrassment. "I want to spend the rest of my life figuring you out. And I think I know what I want to be. I always thought it was professional basketball or nothing, but now I know I want to coach. I want to help other kids see what really matters in life. Like you helped me see what matters. I want to help them feel a bond for each other, help them connect to the team, not play just because it's fun, or because they want to win, but because they want to be the best they can be."

I think I loved Mark more then than I ever had before, and he wasn't even talking to me. I don't know why, but he was a better guy with Branna. Even when she was unconscious, he was better with her. She was right for him. I hadn't been.

"There," said Mom. "That's as much as we can do here. We need to get her to the ambulance now."

"I'll go get it," said Tristan. He didn't wait for Mom to give him the key or anything. He just went.

I watched him run off with my full attention. He moved with incredible athleticism and grace. I had never understood how people could sit and watch running on TV, even marathons, which go on for hours.

But I could watch Tristan for a long time. His hands moved smoothly back and forth at his sides, like the pistons of an engine, never catching, never losing speed. His feet seemed to spring off the ground like a cat's, and then he was bounding up again. He looked for a moment like he was going to keep going up, like a rocket into space. Then he would hit an arc and slowly come back down and start all over again. There was magic in every motion. I had never seen another human run as fast, even in the Olympics.

"Is there some magic you can do to make Branna love me as much as I love her?" Mark asked me in a whisper.

I turned my attention back to him. "Mark, she's been in love with you for months, never saying a word. Without any encouragement. I don't think you need any magical help to make her love you more."

"But what if I don't live up to what she expects? Izzie, I don't want to disappoint her. She's been waiting for so long. What if I'm not enough?"

This was a strange conversation to be having with the guy I'd thought was my boyfriend until this morning, but it all made perfect sense to me now. I knew who I was, and I knew who Mark was, and we weren't meant for each other. I could let him go, and I could feel for him when he talked about loving Branna, because I had Tristan, and I didn't need anything else.

I put a hand on his shoulder. "Mark, you're enough. You're more than enough for her."

We were still like that when Tristan came back in Mom's ambulance. He was driving it straight toward us, over curbs and lawn, debris from the giant, and anything else in his way. The policemen were diving this way and that, but they didn't hold guns on him, because they must have thought he was the ambulance driver—the crazy ambulance driver.

"Has he ever driven a car before?" asked Mark.

I thought the answer to that was probably no. Whatever magic they had in Curvenal, it apparently didn't include the internal combustion engine.

"Are we going to let him drive?" asked Mom.

"You need to be in the back with Branna. And I think

Mark wants to be with her, too," I said. "To talk to her. But I could drive."

Mom shook her head. "No, Izzie, you need to be with us, in case we need your magic for Branna on the drive over. And we're going home, not to the hospital. I need to be able to use potions freely. That's the only thing that's going to save Branna."

"So that leaves Tristan driving," I said.

"I hope we survive," said Mom. "Teenage drivers."

We loaded Branna into the back, and Tristan turned on the siren. I had to hold on, and I was bumped up next to Mark more than once. Even when that happened, though, Mark only had eyes for Branna.

We got to my house, and Tristan pulled into the driveway with a lurch that I thought would send us straight through the garage.

Then he jumped out and opened the back door of the ambulance. He tried to help with Branna, but Mark wouldn't let anyone else carry her.

"Remind me never to drive with you again," I said to Tristan as we went in the front door.

He glanced up at me with a look of hurt in his eyes.

I blew him a kiss. "On the other hand, nothing wrong with the girl driving the guy, is there?"

"Not as far as I know," said Tristan.

There were a lot of things to like about a guy who had grown up a little isolated from the rest of the world. He didn't have set ideas about what I could and couldn't do.

"Good. Did I ever tell you how awesome you are, Tristan?" I asked.

"No, I don't think you have," said Tristan, a little wary.

"Well, you are." I beamed my brightest smile, and I think he started to believe me. He relaxed and I could see him holding himself differently, more upright. Wow. That made him look even hotter.

No time for ogling now, though. We had to help Branna. She didn't look so good anymore. I wasn't even sure if she was breathing.

Mark had laid her out on the couch in the living room. Mom went into the potion cabinet and came back with something that looked pretty grim. It was a muddy greenish gray, and when she pulled out the cork, the potion spat and kicked drops of liquid into the air. One drop touched Mark and he slapped at his arm.

"What is that?" he demanded.

"This is Branna's only hope," said Mom. "It's life itself. Hot and sharp and spitting fire."

I felt a connection to it, like it was made of some part of me. The smell was like rotten eggs, and there was no reason for me to want to touch it, but I did.

"Izzie, let yourself focus. You should activate this, not me. It will be more powerful that way, and more personalized, since you know Branna."

Now was not the time to argue about how well I knew Branna. I'd made mistakes, but she was my best friend, and I still knew her better than anyone else—at least, anyone who could use magic.

Mom handed me the bottle and I felt the heat sear my hand. There was no visible burn on me when I finished, but I could see that the liquid in the bottle had changed color, from gray to amber. I looked up at Mom.

She nodded.

"Now open Branna's mouth, Mark," said Mom.

Obediently, Mark held Branna's mouth open with two fingers.

"And be careful, because if she comes back, she'll bite you." She didn't give any hints about how to prevent that. I guess Mark wouldn't care if he lost a couple of fingers for a good cause. Like reviving his true love.

"Pour, Izzie. Tristan, you hold Branna down. I'm going to get ready to pump her heart back into action, because that first start doesn't always work."

"How much?" I asked.

"Just keep pouring until she starts choking," said Mom.

I took a breath and I poured. A little at first, and then more and more as I became terrified that it was too late, that after everything Branna had done for me, I would fail at saving her.

Tristan muttered some words that sounded half like a song and half like a prayer in that other language, Greek or French or whatever. It was beautiful, and under any other circumstances, I would have kissed him.

If I had to be in a situation like this, I was glad it was with Tristan.

"Mom," I said as I tipped the bottle up and the last few drops fell into Branna's mouth. "She hasn't choked."

"I know, Izzie."

We all knew. It was bad news.

"I'm going to kill someone," said Mark, and then he started sobbing. He let go of Branna for the first time, and her head tilted back.

I didn't know if it was the change in position, or if the potion had just needed time to work, but Branna coughed, and I saw her eyes open for a moment.

Mom put her hands on Branna's chest and started pumping. She didn't do breaths, just the pumping.

Branna's face turned from whitish gray to pink in a few seconds. It was the most amazing thing. It was real magic.

I swore, and then I laughed.

"She's going to be okay!" I shouted. Then I hugged Mark and kissed him, but not in that way. Not a passionate kiss, just one of relief and joy.

Tristan made a funny sound, so I turned and kissed him, too. It wasn't a long kiss, but it was completely different. He had to stop it, and then it took me a few seconds to remember Branna.

Branna, my best friend.

When I was kissing Tristan, everything else tended to fade away.

"Branna, can you hear me? Branna?" I said, taking her hand.

"Here, let me try." Mark nudged me out of the way. He reached for Branna's hands. "Branna, it's me, Mark."

A hand reached for him and then fell back. "Mark," Branna said in a raspy voice.

"Don't let her get up," Mom warned. "She's been through a lot. She needs absolute rest to recover. Once a heart has been dead, it can die again easily in the next few days. And I don't want to have to revive her again."

"You're out of the potion," I pointed out, holding up the bottle.

"There is that, too, and mandrake root is expensive.

Although considering the earthquake and the number of hours I'm probably going to be working this week, we should be fine financially."

"What—what happened?" Branna asked weakly, looking around. "I thought we were at the school. The giant? Don't tell me it was all a dream."

"No, the giant was real," I said. "He must have hit you with a piece of wood and it speared you into the ground."

She put a hand to her stomach and felt along the scar I'd left in her skin. "I can't believe I'm still alive." She glanced at me.

I shrugged.

Mark bent down and kissed the wound. "This is the most beautiful thing I have ever seen, Branna," he said. Then he looked up at her. "You are the strongest, most capable, most amazing woman, and I—" He stopped, apparently speechless.

"Oh," said Branna, like she hadn't expected that. "You're not just saying that because you thought I was dead, are you?"

"No, I'm not just saying because you were dead! I'll say it every minute of every day for the rest of your life if you want. So long as you promise to live a very long life."

"I'll try," said Branna, and she closed her eyes.

"What happened? Is she dead again?" Mark asked frantically. He tried to lift Branna into his arms, but Mom swatted him away, and Mark didn't fight her, although he probably could have thrown her across a football field if he'd wanted to.

Mom bent down and listened to Branna. "She's breathing," she said. "She's just asleep. She's fine. Or she will be, when I'm finished with her."

I sagged forward and Tristan caught me. I was exhausted in a way I didn't think I could be and still be alive. I had lived through an earthquake, used my magic for the first time, killed a giant with fireballs, saved Branna's life, and endured a NASCAR race home to save her again.

I never wanted to do anything heroic ever again. I just wanted to take a bath and put on some clean clothes.

Instead, I called Branna's parents to tell them she was okay and was going to stay at our house overnight. Her mom said that was fine, and she should call them when she was ready to go home.

Chapter 23

Mom bandaged my cuts from the glass and told me she didn't think they would need a healing potion. As for Mark, he tried to resist taking anything Mom gave him, but she reminded him that Branna would have a much harder recovery if she woke up to find her boyfriend dying of sepsis. It turned out he had a ruptured spleen, which I helped fire-seal. Then Mom gave him a magic salve for his burns.

Tristan didn't need anything at all. He had come through the attack unscathed except for a few bruises from his fight with Mark, and Mom didn't argue when he said they didn't hurt.

After all that, I went upstairs and changed out of my disgusting, giant-stink-infested clothes. I bathed without putting my hands or shoulder in the water. Then I put on a nice pair of khakis and a shirt that clung to me in all the right places. Not that I thought Tristan needed to be coaxed to stare at me, but it made me feel more confident. Then I went downstairs.

Branna seemed to be recovering enough to open her eyes and murmur a few words, which was good, and Mark was there beside her. He didn't look at me once, which was fine with me. I hadn't worn the shirt for him.

Mom stood up and turned to Tristan. "You have your sword?" she asked.

He nodded. "I will return to the school," he said.

She seemed to know what he was talking about, but I didn't. "What for?" I asked.

"The giant's magic must be destroyed," said Tristan.

"But I already—" I said.

"You destroyed its body, to protect the non-magical world from discovering the truth," said Mom. "But now the magic of the giant needs to be dissipated."

"Oh," I said, not really understanding.

"And also," Mom added, "I have to get back to the school in the ambulance. There may be others who need me." She checked on Branna once more and told Mark to call her if there was a problem. Then she grabbed her bag of supplies and got back into the ambulance with me and Tristan. She drove this time, and even with the siren on, it felt sedate compared to Tristan's driving.

We got out of the ambulance and saw a long line of people waiting to be treated. Tristan and I had to sneak around a police barrier and keep close to the walls of the school to stay out of sight. We didn't want to be told we had to go back for our own safety. Luckily, the police weren't watching carefully for people coming into the disaster area.

They were paying more attention to people who wanted to get out.

When we got to the pile of ashes that had been the giant's body, no one was paying attention to it, which was good.

Tristan got out his sword.

"It is dead, isn't it?" I asked.

"Dead, but it could be brought back to life with the magic left inside its body." Tristan looked at me gravely. "I have seen it done before. Some years ago, there was a man in Curvenal who was killed, who had magic in his body. He was a sorcerer and he climbed out of his grave, though his wounds were so great that his body would not hold in one piece. Even so, he walked away from his wife, his daughters, and went to serve the serpent. My father was one of the men who went to stop him, and I followed after him."

It was obvious from Tristan's haunted expression that it was not a good memory. "Do you want to talk about it?"

"With you?" he said, shaking his head. "I should not tell you of such terrible things."

"Tristan, I'm not a child, and I'm not a porcelain doll. I'm not going to break if you tell me the hard stuff. I really want to know about your life. All of it." After all, his life was going to be my life soon. "So tell me, what happened when your father went after the sorcerer?" He already knew what had happened when mine had, though I didn't know whether Tristan's father's attempt had taken place before or after Mom and I left Curvenal.

"I was eight years old that day," said Tristan.

So this was after we'd left. After Dad was dead and the serpent was in charge of Curvenal because there wasn't a sorcerer there to stop him.

"My father lost an arm to the serpent." Tristan pointed to his right side, at the elbow. "He could never wield a sword again. He could only teach me what he knew. He watched me practice every day for hours, told me everything I did wrong."

"And you liked that?" It sounded like it, but I knew I wouldn't have liked it if my dad had done the same thing.

"He was protecting me in the only way he knew how," said Tristan. He reached over his shoulder and whispered something, then pulled out the sword, seemingly from nowhere.

It was cool to watch. "Doesn't it get in the way when you're doing other things?" I hadn't noticed him once moving awkwardly because of the sword, even when he was fighting Mark.

"It is not here until I bring it out," said Tristan.

"I don't understand."

"It goes to another place until I call it by its true name."

Another dimension? I remembered my physics teacher talking about the possibilities of multiple universes, a multiverse, and what the mathematical and physical laws in those places would be. It had been hard to believe then, but maybe at a certain point, physics and magic weren't so different.

"What's its name, then? Excalibur or something?" I asked.

"No. That is a different sword. And one that has been misused. This one is still pure."

I waited for him to tell me the name.

"It is Excoriator," he said, moving his lips like he had before but this time making enough sound that I could distinguish the syllables.

It was an intimidating name. "So if that sword cuts off

the giant's head, then the serpent can't bring him back to life?"

"Yes, the magic in the sword's blade sends the giant's soul to hell, and there are angels with similar swords who guard the gates of hell to keep him from returning. The name of the sword also dissipates the magic here on earth."

"Let's do it, then," I said. I definitely wanted to make sure the giant did not return.

Tristan strode forward, not running this time, but with an easy balance despite the weight of the sword.

The giant rubble took up most of one end of the parking lot.

Tristan said the sword's name, then raised it. I heard a sound like a crack of thunder, and the blade came down like lightning. A stench like old fish and garbage dumps spewed out of the giant's head, and I wondered if maybe I shouldn't have bothered changing my clothes. It seemed likely that I was going to have to throw this outfit away, along with the one I'd worn earlier. It was a shame, too, because I really liked the way the khakis fit my butt. I hadn't even had the chance to ask Tristan what he thought.

Clearly, in the future, I was going to have to figure out which times were good for dressing up and which weren't. Otherwise Mom would have to get a second job to support my habit of being attacked by magical creatures.

"I hope there are better times for us ahead," said Tristan, breathing hard. He leaned on the sword before putting it away, just as I heard the sound of a helicopter's blades.

I looked up and saw a channel number painted on the outside and a cameraman hanging out the side.

That was bad.

Had Tristan put the sword away in time? If not, would people think it was just a prop sword? Would anyone realize it was magic?

Mom would have to take care of that, though. Tristan and I had other things to do.

I grabbed Tristan's hand, and we ran around the other side of the school, then over the football field into a neighbor's yard. "We're going to have to walk home from here," I said.

Mom was busy, and I didn't think there was a car worth driving left in the parking lot. Not that any of them were mine in the first place.

"Walking with you will be a pleasure," said Tristan.

I leaned on his arm and we went the long way around. But we had to go up a hill, so when we looked back, we could see the fire engines, ambulances, and police cars.

In the evening newspaper, the lead story was LOCALIZED QUAKE STUNS TINTAGEL HIGH.

Yeah, very localized.

The fire that had devastated the parking lot afterward was attributed to a gas-line break, and it was called "miraculous" that every student and teacher who had been in the building had been accounted for. There were a few minor injuries, but no one had been hospitalized.

I saw the smiling face of my physics teacher and a list of the students he had saved. Good thing he knew the laws of our universe so well.

Nothing about magic, not even a hint. So that meant the

teachers and students at Tintagel were safe—as long as they stayed far away from me.

I didn't see any photos of Tristan with his sword.

When Tristan and I walked through the front door, newspaper in hand, Branna was awake again, drinking some juice. Mom had told Mark not to let her sit up or eat anything solid, despite her complaining loudly about being hungry. Mark just kept kissing her hands and gently touching her face. Then she would look back at him with shining, sappy eyes and quit talking.

"I love happy endings," I said, and I meant it 100 percent. I really was happy for her, and for Mark, too. I had Tristan beside me, and I felt like I had conquered the world and was ready for a rest now.

Unfortunately, that's not what happened.

A couple of hours later, Mom came home. She said she had taken care of the helicopter camera crew, using an amnesia potion in aerosol form. Even though she looked exhausted, she insisted on making us something to eat. "You've got to keep up your strength," she said. "You've all been through a lot today."

"I'm not really hungry," I said.

"Hmm. How about you, Tris?" asked Mom.

"I suppose I could eat a little," said Tristan.

So I went into the kitchen with him, and Mom made us sandwiches. It wasn't until then that I realized I was starving. I guess killing giants takes more out of you than you might think.

I finished one sandwich and another and felt like a pig when I almost finished a third. Mark ate four. But Tristan was on number five when he asked if he could have the rest of mine. I handed it over and watched as he finished off an entire gallon of milk. Mark had gone into the other room to look after Branna by then.

"Well, I was planning to go shopping tomorrow, anyway," said Mom. "I need more potion ingredients. I'll just have to stop at the grocery store, too."

"You eat that much often?" I asked Tristan.

He shrugged. "Magical work takes more energy than non-magical work. I know a man in Curvenal who ate an entire bull after he used magic to build an addition to his house. He and his wife were expecting twins."

I thought suddenly of Tristan as a dad. He would be a good dad. Just like my dad had been. In fact, I wished Dad were here to see him now. He would have been proud.

"So, where are you planning to sleep tonight, Tristan? You should stay over here, unless you have someplace else to go," Mom said.

Tristan shook his head and muttered something about "propriety."

"On the couch," said Mom. "Far away from Izzie. She can lock her door if that would make you feel better."

Tristan went beet red. "Of course, I would never—" he said. But he couldn't bring himself to say any more.

And why was he thinking that he was the only one involved in those kinds of choices, anyway? I had to have a talk with him about that.

"Well, where else are you going to go?"

"I can go somewhere else," said Tristan. "I'll walk."

Now Tristan had a chance to see my mom in her full dragon persona. No magic involved.

"Tristan, you will not walk another step if I have anything to say about it. And I do."

I cleared my throat. "Um, Mom."

"You have no idea, either of you, of the dangers you face. Who's to say that another giant won't come after you? Or something worse? Now that they know where you are, it won't be hard to follow your scent, you know, either of you. Tris, you need Izzie's magic. Izzie, you need Tris's knowledge about magic, and that sword of his doesn't hurt, either."

Now I knew why Mom had been feeding us. She was getting ready to send us out to war, and she wanted to make sure we were leaving on full stomachs.

"Fine," I said. "We get it. Don't we, Tristan?"

He nodded, but he didn't look happy. "I will stay on the front porch," Tristan finally offered.

"On the porch? It's almost winter. It's going to be close to freezing tonight," said Mom.

"I have slept outside through many winter nights," said Tristan with a look of complete honesty. "I will need a few furs."

"We use blankets here," I said. But I didn't think I was going to have any luck convincing him to stay inside.

Even Mark tried to talk Tristan into staying here. Then he called his parents and asked for permission to stay and keep an eye on Branna.

Afterward, I could tell he told them something else, though, because he was smiling softly at Branna.

"What is it?" I asked.

Mark shrugged. "I told my mom that you and I broke up and that I was with Branna now. And my mom said she always wondered about me and Branna, if I would ever notice her. I guess she suspected all along something like this would happen."

"I thought she liked me," I said, pouting a little. I liked Mark's mom. She did judo and she also knew how to make a mean cheesecake.

"Oh, she did. I mean, she does," said Mark. "But she said she thought I wasn't really seeing you, just the girl you wanted me to see. And she thought Branna was hiding behind you. I guess she was right."

I sighed. "Mothers sometimes are," I said, looking at mine.

"Sometimes?" said my mom.

Branna called her parents again and this time told them more of the whole story, that she had been injured during the earthquake, but my mom was taking care her at home.

I could hear them on speakerphone, and her mom said, "It's just as well. From what I hear, the hospital is full anyway. By the way, I don't suppose you've heard from your great-aunt?"

Branna said no, she hadn't and made a funny face at me.

It was a strange question.

"Well, she called," said Branna's mom. "She heard the news story from all the way in Germany and wanted to know if you were all right. Said she had a vision that you were hurt by something very large. Something giant, I think she said. An earthquake could be considered giant, couldn't it?"

I stared at Branna. A vision? About a giant? Maybe she

had magic in her family after all. We'd have to talk about that later.

Mom assured Branna's parents that she would keep an eye on Branna, and there was no need for them to worry.

When she hung up, she checked Branna's scar. "You did an amazing job of healing her, Izzie," she said. "Especially considering the fact that it was your first try."

"Must be all those years listening to you talk about healing," I said.

"I suppose something rubbed off after all."

"Yeah," I said happily. I might not have Mom's magic, but I had her smarts.

Then I got a whole stack of blankets for Tristan and went out to the front porch, where it was starting to turn to twilight. The hammock was still out from the summer. Mom and I sometimes sat out here at sunset, sharing the hammock. Even with the dust from the "earthquake" at the school, the sight had never been more beautiful.

"I'm worried," I told Tristan.

He didn't say anything.

I looked over and realized he had already fallen asleep.

But I also noticed he had his hand on his shoulder, ready to grab the sword and call it to use.

Chapter 24

At two a.m. I heard the thumping of Tristan getting out of the hammock, followed by the ringing of his sword.

I ran out to the porch and saw Tristan standing on the steps as streams of rats, mice, snakes, cats, and dogs came after him. They looked like perfectly ordinary animals, except that they had glowing red eyes and they were attacking Tristan en masse. Or was it the house itself they were after?

When Tristan moved to the side, they would come after me, whoever was closest to the front porch. And they just kept coming, not seeming to feel any fear.

"What are they?" I asked. I started to send fireballs at the animals. But then they got back up again, reanimated.

A squirrel jumped right at my face and I had to beat it off before I remembered I could use a fireball at it. Even after it was dead, I kicked at it to get it out of the way. I was careful to kick at the other ones as soon as they fell dead from my fireballs, too.

I shuddered at the stench that rose around the house, dead animals and fire combined. What was going on?

I remembered Tristan telling me about the man who had gone to serve Gurmun even after he was dead.

If that was what had happened to these creatures, there was no point in attacking them directly.

My stomach clenched, and I thought carefully. Then I tried to focus my magic slightly differently. I made a wall of fire between me and Tristan and the animals. They threw themselves at the fire, but it kept them from getting too close to us—for now.

"Why is Gurmun doing this?" I asked. "Does he think we'll just get tired and let them kill us?"

"I don't know," said Tristan. "Maybe he is just trying to distract us."

"Distract us from what?"

Tristan's eyes shone in the light of the sword. "From going back to Curvenal, where he is," he said.

Right. It was time to live up to what I'd promised. I'd told Tristan I would go back with him. There was no reason for us to wait any longer.

"Let's go, then," I said.

"But what about your mother? And Branna and Mark?" said Tristan.

He was right. We couldn't just leave them to be attacked by the animals.

"I'll wake up my mom. She can use a potion to protect her

and Branna and Mark, and lay a magical poison around the house. Any creature that passes it will die."

"But what if many pass at once?"

"I'll leave up the fire wall," I said. "For as long as I can, anyway." I might not be able to concentrate on it once we got to Curvenal and the real battle started with Gurmun.

"He will know we are coming," said Tristan. "He will be prepared. "

"Then so will we," I said.

When I told Mom everything, and she saw the animals behind the fire wall, she nodded and put her arm around me, tousling my hair. Then she let go and stood up straight.

"I knew this day was coming," she said. "The day I would have to say good-bye to you and trust you to be able to protect yourself. But I am glad that you will have Tris with you."

Her saying his name like that made me wonder if I should start calling him that, too. He said Tantris was his real name, but it was confusing because I had been thinking of him as Tristan for so long. Maybe "Tris" would be a good compromise.

"Wait," Mom said as I turned. "The invincibility potion. You must take that first." All these years, she had felt guilty because Dad had gone off without a working potion to fight Gurmun, and she would not let me do the same thing.

"Good idea," I said.

She went inside and got a small bottle filled with clear, yellow liquid. "Drink half," she said.

I did. It didn't taste too bad. There were hints of ginger and vinegar.

Mom put her hands on my shoulders. "Kill him," she said, a bloodthirsty look in her eye. "Kill him for your father."

"I will, Mom," I said. "I love you."

"I love you, too." She kissed me on the forehead, then nodded to Tristan. "Give the rest of the potion to him."

She went inside.

Tristan drank the rest of the invincibility potion in one swallow, staring at the rampaging animals. I guess he was used to taking potions.

"How long will it take us to get to Curvenal?" I asked.

"Not long," said Tristan, "with Excoriator."

I wasn't sure what he meant, but I trusted him. He wrapped one arm around me and held the sword high with the other. We rose into the air, above the wall of fire. The animals beneath ignored us. Apparently, Gurmun had sent them to a location, not to a particular scent.

At first, the sword took us at a nice pace, more like floating than flying. But the longer I held on to Tristan, the faster we went. I could see houses and farms speeding by beneath us, faster than if we were on an airplane. I suppose the sword protected us from things like birds flying into us. But it didn't protect us from the rain cloud we flew through. We both came out of it soaking wet, and my hands hurt from holding on to Tristan so hard.

By then, I could see mountains in front of us. They were maybe two hundred miles from Tintagel, and I tried to estimate how long it had taken us to get there. Thirty minutes, maybe?

We dropped before we crested over the mountains, and

I saw a lake beneath us. The mountains had snow on them already, and the lake looked awfully cold.

"We're not going to swim through that lake while we hold the sword, are we?" I asked. Was Curvenal a sunken city, like Atlantis? Was that how the magic had stayed so secret?

"Because I don't know how to swim," I added. I didn't mind getting into shallow water, but even with Tristan holding on to me, I would have a panic attack if we had to go underwater. We had taken the potion, but was that enough? Even if there was somehow air under there, I didn't think I could manage it.

"The city is just across the water. On an island," said Tristan. "And we will ride."

The sword let us down gently by a small, narrow rowboat Tristan called a skiff. I took a deep breath and stepped on board. The skiff shifted, and I screamed. I fell into the water, thrashing.

Tristan pulled me out. It was only four inches deep, and I was freezing.

"I'll go first," he said. He stepped into the skiff, then offered me his hand.

I had to swallow back terror, and I thought about how I must have transferred my fear of the serpent to the water. But knowing that didn't help me feel calm.

I sat down, trembling. The skiff was just barely big enough to fit the two of us, if we didn't mind touching knees. Which we didn't. I was glad to have a constant reassurance from Tristan's warm legs, even if they were still damp.

I nodded to him that I was ready, and Tristan put

Excoriator in the water. At first I thought he was going to use it like an oar, but he didn't put pressure on it or draw it through the water. He simply held it, and the water moved around it in great swaths. I held tightly to the sides of the skiff and studied Tristan's chin. He had a great chin line, really. It should be the model for the perfect chin line for guys. If I focused on that, I didn't have to think about the water.

I could almost forget we were headed to face a giant magical serpent who wanted to kill us and the rest of the world.

Until the wind started blowing us off course.

Tristan raised the sword and spoke its name again, then put it back in the water. In just that short time, the skiff had turned around twice, and I had no idea which direction we were headed in anymore. It felt like we were surrounded by water and would never escape.

Waves began to slosh into the skiff. I saw my fingers turning blue as I held on to the wooden sides, and Tristan was leaning forward at the other end, holding the sword in the water as firmly as he could. I was too cold and scared to make any noise, and I kept telling myself we had taken an invincibility potion, so we would be fine.

It felt like we were caught in a hurricane, even though I knew that wasn't possible. But I also knew that the serpent, Gurmun, had a lot of magic. If he didn't want us to reach him, he would do everything in his power to stop us. Even Tristan was shuddering, and his teeth were chattering, as the skiff twirled around. Just when I thought we were going to fall into the water, there was a sudden thunk and the skiff cracked.

I was sure this was the end.

Tristan pulled me upright and then walked with me right out of the skiff and onto land. There were a few deserted buildings ahead of us, one that looked like a burned-out shed, and another that might have been five or six stories high but was now just a skeleton. The others were too far away for me to see distinguishing features, but I smelled ash in the air, and everything seemed dingy and old.

Nothing to worry about here, I thought.

I started to cry and almost fell down in relief. Tristan pulled me close—so close that I could feel the rush of blood in his forehead, pounding in rhythm with my own; so close that I could taste his lips, his sweat; so close that I could feel the hard bone of his nose as it pushed on my cheek.

It wasn't a kiss. A kiss is what happens when you feel in love and you want to share that joy with the other person. Or when you feel the heat of passion, and you want to tease and play and be played with in return. There was no happiness in this moment of need, no pleasure, no joy. Tristan and I were pressed against each other and made into one body, one soul. We wouldn't have survived otherwise.

Finally, Tristan put the sword away.

"Gurmun," he said. And he nodded at something ahead of us.

I looked and could see nothing but the sun over the ruined buildings. It had grown very large and bright enough that I had to turn away from it or squint.

Then the sun started to move, and it got larger and larger. And I realized it was not the sun after all. It was a serpent with eyes that burned as brightly as two suns and with scales of red and yellow and orange, with hints of blue at the edges, like the center of a flame, where there is the most heat. It was the serpent from my worst nightmare, only it was real.

Chapter 25

Though it was huge, the serpent didn't make the ground shake as it approached, simply because it had no legs. Instead of stomping like the giant, it slithered closer, its scales cutting smoothly and soundlessly through the sand. It was really long—so long I couldn't see the end of its tail—and the power of its magic was unmistakable. The magic shimmered all around the scales like light, but it was invisible, like when you see steam rising off the sidewalks, and your vision is just a little distorted.

The head glared down at Tristan and me, and then it swooped.

I leaped back and put a hand to my throat. But the serpent's head was in my face, and it breathed on me. The scent was anger and smoke.

"So you are the one with the great magic," said the serpent. It was the first of the magical creatures I had met that spoke any sort of normal English with intelligence. I was not under any illusion about that being a good thing.

The serpent's head moved slowly, inch by inch, around my face, its forked tongue slithering out to smell me.

"Tristan," I said softly.

He took my hand in his. "Just be calm. He's trying to frighten you so you don't think before you use your magic."

The serpent *was* frightening me, but I hadn't used my magic yet. So did that mean I was winning?

"I am Gurmun," said the serpent.

What nice manners it had, for a serpent.

"Uh. Gee. N-Nice to meet you," I stammered.

"And you are Isolde."

"Don't say your name to him," said Tristan.

"Why not?"

"He can use it to find your magical source and steal from it. The sound of your own voice saying your name is the most powerful key to magic." Was that why Tristan had been so careful about not using his full, true name at school?

"But he told me his," I said.

Gurmun was now sniffing the other side of my head. It felt creepy, that tongue darting out and touching my bare neck, or an earlobe.

"Only part of his name," said Tristan. "No one knows what his full name is. Or how to say it exactly the right way."

There must be a special way of saying my name, too, I thought. But if I didn't know what it was, who did?

Gurmun's whole body had curved, so I could see how thick he was at the top. He was as wide as the forty-year-old oak tree by the school. He coiled around me, only millimeters away from touching me.

I couldn't think about names right then. I had to make myself breathe normally, because I felt like I was in an enclosed space that was getting smaller and smaller, and soon the serpent would simply tighten his coils and I would be crushed.

"I eat my victims living," said Gurmun as his head came around the other side of me. "I like to hear them scream while I take their magic and their lives."

My feeling of being trapped was worse than ever.

Why had we come here?

What had made me think that I could defeat this serpent?

Tristan and I should have run away from Tintagel when the animals attacked my mom's house. We should have kept running. At least then we might have stayed alive.

"So, did you enjoy the taste of death the slurg gave to you?" Gurmun's head weaved down until his eyes were level with mine.

I blinked fast and felt tears running down my cheeks from the pain of staring at him.

"Shield yourself," said Tristan. "Or look away."

But I would not. Gurmun might kill me, but he wouldn't cow me.

"Thank you," I said.

Gurmun blinked, and I had a brief respite from the light of his eyes. Then he grimaced. "What do you mean?" he asked, his tongue slipping out and licking the length of my face, from my forehead, over my eye, down to my chin and neck. "Why do you thank me?"

I refused to tremble or falter. "I did not know I had magic

until you sent the slurg to me. You helped me discover who I was. And for that I thank you."

"So that is why it has been so difficult to find you. You are new to your magic, and you come against me anyway. Ah, the brave always die well, even if they are foolish." The serpent's head rippled, and he made a strange hissing sound that I realized was his version of laughter.

Gurmun knocked me over with his head.

I fell into the water, panicking because I wasn't sure which way was up. I thrashed in the water, my lungs on fire. But then I remembered what Tristan had said. Be calm.

I let my arms go out, and then I floated up to the surface. When my head came out of the water, I took a few strokes and found myself on the sand again. The wind blew into my face, and I shivered, but I stood tall. "Is that all you have?" I asked Gurmun, hands at my hips.

He slithered closer.

"Isolde, be strong!" shouted Tristan. He was standing with his sword held high, waiting for the right moment.

Gurmun wrapped himself around me and began to squeeze. "You like to be held tight by the little warrior, don't you? You believe in love conquering all, just as your father did, I suppose?"

"Yes." I got the word out, but it was the last one I spoke. As he pressed me harder and harder, I could feel my ribs begin to strain. I knew from Mom that if they broke, the real danger was a punctured lung. But broken bones wouldn't kill me, as long as I could deal with the pain.

I stirred up a fireball and concentrated so that I could send it from my eyes to Gurmun's.

He let go of me in that instant.

"I see you have some of your father's power," he said, and pulled back.

I was feeling pretty good about myself then, able to send fireballs however I wanted. "And my mom's invincibility potion," I said.

"Oh?" said Gurmun.

Knowing that Tristan and I had drunk the potion had given me a sense of distance from the serpent's power. Dad hadn't had the potion, but we did. So whatever Gurmun did to us, he couldn't kill us, right?

"You think a witch's potion will work against me?" said Gurmun. Then he spat at me.

The saliva felt warm at first, and then it began to burn. I heard a sizzle, and when I looked down, I saw some faint smoke rising from my skin. I tried to shake off the spit, but it was too thick and viscous. Where I shook myself, it seemed to cling even more.

Gurmun hissed, laughing. Then he reared up and moved more quickly than I would have thought possible. In a moment, he had spat on Tristan, as well.

"Tristan?" I said.

"It's his magic. It is eating your mother's potion," Tristan said to me.

Had he known beforehand that this could happen? Why hadn't he told me? Why had he even bothered to take the potion in the first place? It had gotten us here, but what good was that? Maybe it would have been better to die in the storm while we'd crossed the lake. Then I wouldn't have had to look into Gurmun's triumphant eyes.

"Now you are stripped down to your true self," said Gurmun. "How does it feel?" He bent down, coiled around me, and once again tried to crush me.

I was finished with being calm and holding back. I didn't even think about using magic. I just hit him in the face with my fist and started kicking at him.

His eyes looked startled, and he made some low sounds of pain. He began to uncoil from me.

I focused and sent a fireball into his face. I heard him scream loudly; it was a sound that seemed to reverberate into the ground.

"Isolde, don't be fooled!" Tristan called to me.

I had been leaning forward to see what damage I had done, but I pulled back just in time. Gurmun snapped at my arm.

I think he would have sheared it off. Instead, he took only the tip of one of my fingers.

I felt faint just seeing the dripping blood. But I shook it off and stood tall.

Gurmun was not damaged at all.

"Shall I take you bit by bit?" asked Gurmun, looming closer again. "A delicious meal you would make that way, many small courses to heighten the anticipation of the final one, the dessert—your death."

"Do what you will!" I challenged him.

"Isolde!" cried Tristan. He ran toward me and shook me. "He is still trying to frighten you. You have not used even the smallest part of your magic here."

"Has she not?" said Gurmun disdainfully.

"Isolde, he has been afraid of you since you were born. He knows that you are more powerful than he is. That is why he killed your father and why he has been seeking you out ever since."

Then Gurmun's head bent down to Tristan, and he seemed genuinely angry for the first time. "Little warrior. You think either of you will survive another moment if I do not wish it?"

"Yes, I do!" exclaimed Tristan.

"Do you not know that I allowed you to leave Curvenal? That I sent others to track you, because I believed you would be my best hope of finding the girl with magic?"

Tristan's sword arm began to droop. "No," he whispered.

"But now you have come back and brought her with you. In the end, you have been as much a servant of mine as the slurg or the giant—more so, I think."

Tristan gritted his teeth and shoved his sword toward Gurmun.

The serpent moved out of the way.

"Tristan, don't listen to him!" I said. He could not let Gurmun beat him before the battle had begun.

"Try to prick me with that pin of yours," Gurmun said to Tristan. "See who it hurts, you or me." Gurmun opened his mouth and showed his teeth. They were all sharp and even, thousands of them in parallel rows, on his upper and lower jaws.

Tristan swung Excoriator and missed again.

I heard the sound of the sword cutting through air.

Gurmun hissed, then lifted his head and positioned his body closer to Tristan. "Right there," he said, pressing a thick part forward. "Try that. That will surely hurt me."

"Tristan, don't," I called out, sure that it was some trick.

But Tristan wouldn't listen. He stabbed with all the force he had. I saw the muscles in his shoulders working and the effort in his face as he brought the sword down.

The weapon clanked and bounced off the serpent's scales, and Tristan had to run to retrieve it.

Gurmun made his hissing laugh again. "Now what have you learned, little warrior?" he asked Tristan. "Put that away. Someone might get hurt. Someone human, that is."

My heart felt as if it had fallen into my stomach. Now there really was only my magic left, and nothing left to distract Gurmun.

But Tristan did not give up easily. He took the sword and moved slowly, his shoulders hunched as if in defeat. I caught a glimpse of his eyes shining and felt a moment's hope.

He got close enough to the serpent that he could stab with the sword again, and did, this time not directly onto the scales but between them.

Gurmun flinched, and a quiver ran up and down the length of his body. Then he began to scream. Black bile poured out of his mouth, and his head fell to the ground, flopping this way and that in the sand.

Tristan removed the sword with a jerk. Then he stuck it in again.

The serpent writhed and screamed even more loudly. Birds flapped past us in black clouds. The lake water rose in high waves that pounded the shore.

Tristan pulled out the sword again.

The serpent did not move.

There was a long moment when I stared, waiting for more.

But there was no sign of life in Gurmun, and when Tristan kicked at him, the serpent's carcass only slipped to one side, its mouth lolled open.

"You did it!" I said. I rushed toward Tristan and put my arms around him. I could not believe it. I hadn't had to use my magic! Maybe Tristan was the one who had been meant to do this all along. Curvenal was his home, after all. He belonged here. He knew Gurmun better than I did.

I was glad I had been here to see it, and glad that Tristan had been able to kill Gurmun with one stroke. One really good stroke.

I looked at the tip of my finger and saw that it was already starting to heal. We were going to be fine now.

But Tristan shook his head slowly. "Something is wrong."

"What is it?"

Tristan would have to cut off Gurmun's head, but I was certain he could do that if he got in under the scales around the scruff of the serpent's neck.

"It was too easy," he said.

"Easy?" I thought about the storm and Tristan's first attempt and Gurmun's laugh. "It wasn't easy. He was just overconfident, that's all."

"You think he knew I could cut between his scales, and he just thought I wouldn't make a second attempt?"

"You're a human. You're smart. He wasn't. He underestimated you."

"Or I underestimated him," said Tristan. We both stared as the serpent began to lift his head once more, and his whole body rose to tower above us.

"You killed me. Congratulations, little warrior," said Gurmun. "Now you can go on your way and have your celebration. And leave the real magic one here with me to finish the job."

He had been faking! We hadn't done anything to him at all. The battle was only just begun.

Chapter 26

Tristan stood at my side, groaning in despair. "But—" I said. "But—" This wasn't possible. Tristan had killed the serpent. Hadn't he?

"Death cannot stop me," said Gurmun. "Your father learned that. I am surprised he did not tell you. Oh, but I killed him before he could speak to you again, didn't I, little magic one?" He shook himself, and I heard the swooshing sound of his scales sliding against each other.

That was a sound I never wanted to hear again.

"Your father was a very powerful elemental sorcerer. I told him as he lay dying that I would come after you. I told him that I would kill you slowly, and you would cry out for death from me as a mercy, that you would beg me like a child begging a father for a gift."

No wonder Mom had taken me away from Curvenal as soon as she could and had kept me away. No wonder she had never told me about my magic. No wonder I had not wanted it back myself for so many years.

Gurmun was trying to make me angry, and he was succeeding. I was so mad that I could feel the heat inside me rise from the pit of my stomach into my throat. Soon it would be coming out of my ears. But I couldn't let go of it yet. I wasn't ready. I didn't know how to kill Gurmun. Not permanently, anyway.

"I can see that your father has been gone too long. There must be someone else you love enough that you would do anything to keep him safe from me?"

I glanced at Tristan. It was stupid, but I couldn't stop myself from giving away that tiny reaction.

Gurmun took full advantage. He might have done it anyway, but I felt it was my fault when he plucked Tristan off the sand beside me and held him in his teeth. Tristan had taken the invincibility potion, but I was sure its power had already been destroyed by the serpent's spit.

Tossing him this way and that, Gurmun swung his body around me as if to give me the best view of Tristan's plight.

"Please," I said. "Please. Put him down."

Gurmun's eyes seemed to grow brighter.

"I'll do anything," I said. "Just let him go."

"Isolde, don't—" Tristan said, and then bit off the words as the serpent tossed him, spinning, into the air and caught him before he fell to the ground, this time on the other side so that I could see the wounds the teeth had made along the top half of Tristan's body. Now, with the potion burned away, his shoulders, neck, and side were purple and bleeding, likely poisoned.

I had to do something to help him.

"If you kill him, you'll have nothing to hold against me. I won't care if I live or die!" I shouted.

Gurmun gradually stopped moving and slowly, almost gently, put Tristan back on the ground, on his feet next to me.

I could hardly believe that he had done what I'd asked. I felt a surge of relief, followed immediately by icy fear.

I looked up at Gurmun.

He hissed. "As you wish," he said. Then the serpent withdrew a few feet.

Tristan slumped forward, his hands outstretched. "I can't see," he said. "Isolde, I'm blind."

There were tooth marks around his eyes and on the rest of his face. The poison from the serpent's teeth must have seeped into his eyes. His other wounds weren't as bad as I had been afraid of, mostly superficial. But he was blind, and he stumbled, letting go of his sword. It dropped to the sandy shore, and he stepped on it clumsily.

But I did not trust myself to try the sword. That was his magic, not mine. I put out a hand to steady Tristan, and it trembled against his skin.

"Isolde," he whispered.

"I'm here."

"Don't leave me," he said.

It broke my heart to hear him. Gurmun really did know how to hurt humans. He wasn't like the slurg or the giant, who just wanted to kill. Gurmun wanted power over us, and to get that, he had to terrorize us. He'd been doing it to Curvenal since he had woken. He would do it to all the world if he had the chance.

I had to stop him. Now that I knew what he was, I wasn't tempted to run away anymore. This was evil that had to be faced.

"I can't see," said Tristan. "It's all black. And it hurts." He pressed his hands to his eyes.

"I know. I'm sorry." I didn't know what else to say to him. I kissed one of his hands and then the other. Then I bent forward and kissed his eyes. "I love you," I said.

"But I'm useless this way. I can't use the sword. I can't do anything."

"You're not useless," I said. "Not to me."

"You don't need a blind man at your side. You need a warrior."

"No." I shook Tristan, hard enough that he winced. But I wanted him to have to hear me, to pay attention. "Gurmun thinks you are only a warrior. He thinks he has defeated you. But he hasn't."

"He has," said Tristan. "He has."

"You are still the one I love," I said. "And I always will."

In that moment, I suddenly knew the truth. All this time, I thought that I had been forced to love Tristan because of the love philtre. But had it been a love philtre? I had poured the love potion I'd made from the Internet recipe down the sink because I knew it didn't have any real magic. And the other one?

In my mind's eye, I could see Mom's potion cabinet. The bottle I had taken out—it had smelled exactly like the invincibility potion that Mom had given us before we came to Curvenal to face the serpent. Sweet and gingery, with a hint of vinegar. In that tiny yellow bottle. That was why the invincibility potion had been so familiar to me when I helped Mom activate it.

Mom had always told me that she was uncertain about love philtres. She had decided not to send the one she made to her friend's daughter because it would take away choice. So why would she keep something that dangerous in her cabinet? She wouldn't. But she would keep an invincibility potion—and that would explain why Tristan and I had survived the slurg's attack.

As for falling in love with Tristan, that fever-hot feeling I'd had when I first met him had nothing to do with a love philtre. It had been my magic recognizing Tristan's. The fire part of my elemental sorcery.

All those years of unconsciously hiding my magic for fear of the consequences had ended. I had known from the beginning that Tristan was the one person to whom I could show my true self. That was why I'd fallen in love with him immediately. The love philtre—really the invincibility potion—had just been a coincidence. And then an excuse.

"Isolde, I can't help you against him," said Tristan. He was holding my arm and trying to sense where Gurmun was, but Gurmun was teasing him, snorting in one direction and then moving to the other before Tristan could respond.

"You can. Tristan, where's your sword?" I said. I loved him. I would always love him. And whether he or I had magic after this wouldn't change that.

"It does not matter. I cannot wield it."

"You can hold it," I said. "Trust me." I would not let him feel like a failure, not now.

Tristan knelt down and began to dig in the sand.

I thought how lucky I was that we had found each other. I had been as blind as he was, in a completely different way.

Tristan found his sword at last. I could hear it humming as he touched it.

"Now what?" he asked.

"I want you to run at Gurmun with it," I said loud enough for Gurmun to hear, but soft enough for him to think I was whispering. I thought Tristan would argue with me. He had already tried that, and it hadn't worked.

"And then what?" he asked.

"And then I want you to give up. Fall down in despair. Tell Gurmun to kill you, that your life is no longer worth living if you cannot wield your sword and use your magic to protect the one you love." I was holding tightly to him, hoping he knew I didn't mean for him to believe this. But on the other hand, maybe it was better if he did believe it. Or if the serpent believed he did.

"This is what you wish me to do?"

"Yes," I whispered, letting go of his arm.

"Then I will do it. When I am gone, I hope that you will find love again."

He really did believe that I was sending him to his death. I should— No, I couldn't. I let him go.

"Gurmun—do your worst!" he cried, and slashing his sword in front of him, he moved stalwartly forward.

Gurmun hissed with laughter and darted this way and that while Tristan tried to react to him.

I felt sick with anger and fear. What was I thinking, doing this to him?

But he had brought me here, to face this challenge. If he believed in me, I must also believe in him.

Tristan leaped toward Gurmun, and the serpent ducked underneath him, unmooring him. I saw him fall, silently, and roll to the side.

"Kill me," said Tristan. "I have no reason to live without my love."

I believed he believed it. How could Gurmun not?

I wept real tears, and I held my breath, waiting to see if he was still alive, but there was no sign of it.

"You are so cruel," I cried out, though I thought I was the one who was cruel. I twisted my hands around and held my head low. "How can you do this to us?"

"How can I not?" said Gurmun. His head came down closer, just as I'd known it would.

Then he began to let his tongue out, to sniff me. Oh, how he loved the smell of grief and pain and hopelessness. That was proof of his power.

I let myself feel the real despair that was all around me, that Tristan had felt just a moment before. It couldn't be fake. Gurmun had to believe it, and he wasn't going to be fooled by crocodile tears. He had to taste the depth of my feelings.

My magic seeped out in dark wisps around me, like smoke signals from a covered fire.

Gurmun murmured to himself and drank it in.

He came closer.

And closer.

"Tell me about my father," I said. "At the end of his life." And I kept up the sense of fear.

Dad had died so that I would live. And I had to believe he'd known that I would return here someday, that I would face Gurmun as he had—and that this time, Gurmun would lose. Like my father, I had the elemental magic that was the only hope for defeating Gurmun, and Mom couldn't protect me from my duty forever. Dad must have left something to help me.

But where? On the shore somewhere? In one of the buildings? Were there others on the island who might know?

He couldn't have depended on any of the buildings being left, or on me finding the people.

I thought desperately, and then I realized that whatever it was, my father had to have left it with either me or Gurmun—in our memories.

"If you wish to see his final despair, I can give you that," said Gurmun.

To my surprise, Gurmun sent me a magical flash of memory, directly from his eyes to my mind.

I saw my father as I had seen him in my dream when I was little. But he was clearer, and there were things I had forgotten that I saw again and knew I had seen before.

My dad was very tall and strong, and he wore gloves and a leather breastplate. His hair was just starting to gray around the temples, and it was curly where he was sweating. His eyes were dark and full of love. I could sense his magic, as Gurmun had sensed it that day, and it was based on fire and on all sources of light: the sun, the stars, and the moon.

My father put up his hands. "I surrender, Gurmun," he said. "Your magic is greater than mine. I surrender my life." He sounded despairing, and I could see Gurmun coming closer and closer to him, as he had with me. Dad was wounded in one leg and was holding his weight off it. Gurmun's teeth had dug into it, and so had his fire.

And even as Dad stood there, Gurmun blew more fire at him. "You puny human, you thought your fire could defeat mine? When my magic was fueled by hundreds of years of anger?"

"I was foolish," said Dad. "Arrogant in my own magic, and ignorant of you and your past. These past hours have tutored me as nothing else has, great Gurmun."

Gurmun hissed at this, pleased. "Your kind should never have sought to chain the true great ones of magic. And now you will pay. You and all those like you." The serpent's fire roared around my father, but Dad's fire weakly fought it back.

"And that is what your father was like," said Gurmun to me now, calling me from the foggy past of remembrance. "A coward in the end. Just like you and your beloved will be."

But I did not come fully out of the link between us. With all the strength in my magic, I clung to the memories he had opened up to me, and pressed further in, insistent on seeing more. Because there had to be a reason that Gurmun had ended it there, before Dad died. That was my only hope.

"What?" muttered Gurmun. "You cannot—"

But obviously, I could, and I did. He had made himself vulnerable by drinking in my despair. Now I drank in his memories.

I could see my father writhing on the ground in agony. He was on a sandy shore just like this one. I thought I could even see the same buildings in the distance, although they were newer then, without a hint of destruction.

I heard scuffling sounds against the rocks that rose above the shore. That must have been my mom coming to get me.

I heard a whispered voice and then a child's cry of refusal. And then the scent of my mother's magic was in the air, lightly.

She must have used it to drug me, to make me sleep so that she could take me away. I would not have wanted to leave my dad in such danger.

"Stop!" said Gurmun distantly, in the present.

But I pushed him away and stayed in the past.

I saw my dad shake himself and get to his feet. He turned to Gurmun, and his back was straight. His body was ravaged by wounds and magic, but he looked the serpent in the eyes. "I will die today, but my daughter will live to see you dead. My daughter, who has magic to match yours, fire for fire."

Gurmun whirled around and saw that I was missing. He roared in anger, turning to my father with glittering eyes. "Your daughter might as well be dead already. She is tiny, vulnerable. I will send out every creature I have for her. She will never survive to understand her magic."

"You do not know my wife. She is strong, and she loves my daughter as I do."

"Your wife is only a witch," sneered Gurmun. "She can do nothing for your daughter."

"Oh, you are wrong. Very wrong. But if you are so sure of yourself, Gurmun, then tell me your name. Your true name. Let me hear it as you would say it yourself."

Gurmun bent down, and through his eyes I could see my dad become larger until he filled the serpent's vision. I could see that he was blind, and that his hands had been scorched, as well. His face was blistered and blackened with soot and dirt. But he winked. At Gurmun.

He winked in the same way he had winked at me when I was little and he'd caught me doing something I knew I shouldn't do. He would wink at me and then say nothing, as if to show that he trusted me.

I remembered it now, though I had tried to suppress a lot of my memories about my dad, because they were too painful to keep hold of.

But why would he wink at Gurmun like that?

Unless he was winking at me, in the memory, knowing that one day I would see it as he meant me to. He had known that when I came back to Curvenal, Gurmun would want to taunt me with his death. My father had saved this memory for me, the weak link in Gurmun's armor.

"This is not—" I heard Gurmun say as he tried to fling me out of his mind, but it did not work.

I continued to see into his memory.

"Or are you afraid of me? A man who is nearly dead and whose only child is a girl but five years old? A frail, little human thing who has barely the first idea of what magic is?" taunted Dad.

Gurmun flashed fire at him again, and Dad's hair was singed, and the leather on his breastplate began to smoke. He did not bother to try to extinguish it.

"No, you stupid human," said Gurmun in the present. "No!"

But it was too late. This had all happened eleven years earlier. It had been waiting for me until I was ready, until I myself understood love and how it could never truly despair.

"I will tell you, human. Because I am afraid of neither of you, now or in the future." Gurmun in the past inhaled, and then, breathing fire, he said, "Gurmun," with a ringing sound that shook the whole earth as the giant had shook the school. It lasted for a long time, ten seconds at least, and my dad closed his eyes in pain at the sound, but he did not cover his ears.

"Thank you," he said. And he fell down, dead.

I let go of Gurmun's mind then and found my own brief memories of that day, when Dad had left me in the cave. I could see his face in my mind and hear his voice as he called me Isolde, three syllables, with a distinct accent that reminded me very much of Tristan's. My true name, I thought. Tristan had always said my true name the right way.

"What a sentimental scene that was," said Gurmun mockingly. "Are you glad that you saw it once before you died?"

"I am glad that I saw," I said. Then I lifted my head and stared into Gurmun's shining bright eyes with all my fire in my own eyes. "But I am not going to die. It is you who will die!"

I roared at him, using my magic to make the sound ring and to make fire billow out of my mouth as he had done. I made exactly the same sound that Gurmun had made, and I saw Gurmun shudder as he recognized his true name.

I moved toward Tristan and helped him pick up his sword once more.

"I am here," I said. "And this is the last of the serpent. You have only to trust me." But would he, after what I had told him? Had he known that it was a feint to fool Gurmun, and not him? Had he believed I would never tell him to give up his faith in me?

The moment I waited seemed very long.

And then. "I trust you," said Tristan in a voice that was soft, but strong.

"Now hold me," I said. "And hold up your sword."

Tristan put one arm around me. With the other he put up his sword.

We were both still wet, smelling of fire, and he was wounded, blind, and staggering upright. But I had never been so happy or so certain of the future.

I used his sword to reflect and intensify my fire magic, and sent it over and over again to Gurmun.

Fire cannot destroy fire, but fire can destroy flesh, and it can destroy a true name. Once those two things were gone, Gurmun's fire was left without a source.

His body had been incinerated. The flakes of it swirled around us, adding to the ashy smell and the gritty residue covering the whole island.

I guided Tristan toward the place where the serpent's head would have been.

"Is this the right place?" I asked.

He closed his eyes, trying to feel for it, I guess. I didn't know if it would work, but suddenly, he stabbed forward, and I could feel that things had changed, that there was something missing that had been there before.

Tristan held up his arm, shaking with the weight of the sword.

"I think you can let go of me now," I said.

He shook his head. "I don't think I can. Not now, nor ever after."

We kissed then, and it was a kiss full of fire and magic. But mostly, it was a kiss full of love, because when magic is gone, love still lives on.

Chapter 27

There was nothing near us but the sound of the waves sliding gently back and forth against the shore. The horizon was just beginning to turn pink with sunset. The sand was still warm, but I wanted nothing more than to go home, take another bath, and go to bed in my own room, where Mom could watch over me.

Only I had no idea how we were going to get there.

Our skiff was in splinters. Whatever other ships had once been here were gone now, or in pieces. And I saw no sign of people. Tristan had grown up here, so they had to be somewhere. I didn't blame them for not coming out. Gurmun must have kept them terrified all these years, and even if they could feel his magic gone, how could they be sure? He had died at least once that I knew of, and then come back.

"Tristan? Can you hear me?" I asked.

He was breathing shallowly, and his face was pale. I put

my hand to his throat to feel for his pulse. It was there, but it wasn't strong. Every time it skipped a beat, I held my breath. I had to get him back to my mom. I didn't know if she could heal his blindness, but I knew that he had no chance otherwise. I could live with him being blind if I had to, but I didn't know if he could. The warrior thing and all that.

I stood up and shouted, "Help! Is anyone out there?"

There was no response.

I looked up at the rocks, and I realized that I was only a few feet from the cave where I had been hidden by my father. I had a flash of memory that was my own. I had been standing over there when Gurmun rose up against my father. I had screamed and put my hands over my eyes. It had been different then. The smell, the sounds, the whole feeling of the place. It had seemed alive to me then, and now it seemed deserted, very close to death.

Gurmun had brought it to this, and I did not know if it would ever recover. But there was magic here. Other elemental sorcerers, perhaps, and those with metal magic like Tristan and witches like my mother, and maybe some with other kinds of magic I had not even heard about yet. If I had not been so tired, I would have been curious.

But for now, I was worried about Tristan. I had to get him help, and I had to do it immediately. I crouched down, knees bent, back straight. Taking a deep breath, I grabbed Tristan's arms and tucked myself under his body. I lifted him and staggered around for a few seconds. Then I felt the burn in my legs. It was a good thing Tristan wasn't as heavy as Mark.

I tried to use my magic for help, but the fire just made us both hotter, and once I was carrying Tristan's weight, I was plenty hot and dripping sweat. On the other hand, I liked the feeling that I was capable of carrying my boyfriend.

At least, until I tripped on a seashell, got it embedded in my heel, and almost dropped Tristan on his head.

But I didn't, and that's the important part.

I got past the old buildings and the rocks, where I could smell the last ashes of Gurmun in the air. Just beyond that, I stopped and took a rest. I was afraid of letting go of Tristan, because I wasn't sure that once I did, I would ever be able to get him up again. But I was also afraid that my heart was going to beat out of my chest, so I let him fall slowly and made sure there were no rocks under him when he hit the sand.

He opened his eyes for a second when he thunked down. "Oof," he said, and then he was unconscious again.

I sat and rested. The sun was setting, and it was getting colder. I knew I could build a fire when I needed to, but for now, I just sat down, put my head on Tristan's chest, and listened to the beautiful sound of him breathing. Living.

"Tantris, Tantris!" I heard voices shouting.

It took me a moment to remember that was Tristan's real name.

Then I sat up as a dozen people approached us. A woman came forward and offered Tristan a water bottle. She was dressed in worn polyester hip-huggers that might once have had flowers embroidered onto them. Her top was loose and flowy, more gray than white. I wondered how long it had been since anyone in Curvenal had had contact with the non-magical world.

"I'm Isolde," I said.

The woman's eyes went wide. "You give us your name?" she said. "Your true name?"

Whoops. I'd forgotten that might be dangerous. But I hadn't said it the way my dad and Tristan had. I'd used the two-syllable pronunciation that I was used to being called by everyone at home who didn't know me well enough to call me Izzie. It was strange that I had two names, one that people knew me by, and one that I knew myself by, but I guess it was that way for Tristan and everyone else in Curvenal.

"There is no more need to worry about Gurmun, the serpent," I said. "I have killed him, permanently this time, using the magic of his name. With Tristan's, help, of course. I mean, Tantris. You're all safe now." At least, they were safe from Gurmun. I didn't know if there were other slurgs or giants around, but Gurmun must have kept a lot of them away while he was here. Curvenal might have to deal with them in following days but the magic they had here would probably be sufficient to deal with the smaller dangers that might come into the vacuum the serpent had left.

The woman started to cry. "Tantris did it. He did what he said he would do!" she said. "We all thought he would never return, but we should have known he had honor, like his father before him."

A man dressed in an old jean jacket kissed my hand over and over again. "Isolde," he said. His accent, like the woman's, was similar to Tristan's. Maybe it was an older kind of English, closer to the true language of magic. Other people started to close in, patting me on the back, touching my hair, saying things I only half understood. Then a little girl came running up and handed me a doll. It was a homemade doll, crocheted from yarn, with a crooked face and ragged hair.

"For you," she said precisely.

I tried to give it back to her. I looked up and could see more of the town. The houses were small and looked like they hadn't been painted in ages. Maybe they had depended on magic to keep things nice, until the serpent came and took that, too. The doll must be the nicest thing the girl owned. How could I take that from her? I looked up at the woman, and she had her arm around the girl. "Take it," the woman said. "I will make her another one."

So I took it. I'd never been a hero before. It felt good, and also a little scary. I wondered what else they might think I could do. Make it summer all year round? Turn rain into money falling from the sky?

It sure looked like they could use money here.

I searched through my pockets and tried to take out some cash to hand to the mother, but she shook her head. "The serpent took much of our wealth," she said, "and many people have left Curvenal. Now he is gone, we will have no problems. With our magic, we can build new homes, new schools, and people will come back."

I nodded. They were on their way, then. I could think about Tristan now. "I need to get Tristan home to my mother. She's a witch, and I think she might be able to cure his blindness," I said. "Or do you have witches here? There was magic everywhere here, wasn't there?"

"Witches, yes. But witches who can cure blindness from a serpent's poison, no. Your mother was always the best witch in Curvenal. We were very sad when she left us," said the woman.

So Mom was the only one who could help Tristan. "We came here on a skiff, but it's ruined. Are there any other ships? Or planes? Or . . . something else?" I didn't know what, but I was hoping for something fast. I only knew we were far from home, and Mom always said her magic worked best if it was started as soon as possible.

"Isolde?" Tristan whispered.

I knelt beside him.

"You should go back," he said. "With a black sail."

"Why? What difference does it make if the ship has a black sail?" I asked.

"Not that kind of black sail. The people of Curvenal will help you." Tristan insisted on getting to his feet, but he was still blind and weak. One of the men put an arm around him and helped him move farther up the hillside. I followed.

Now I could see dozens of smaller houses that had not been destroyed and the ruins of larger ones. It looked like a place that might have been a vacation community in the summer, so close to the shore and far away from the rest of the world. Maybe it would be like that again, and those people who had left would come back. I saw only a couple of hundred people. There might be more who were hanging back, but if all the ruined buildings had been inhabited at one time, the town had to have been twenty times larger than it looked now.

We passed a fenced-in area, and I expected to see animals in it, but there weren't any. It smelled of Gurmun, and I realized with a sick sensation that it had been a cage for his victims. Everyone else looked away from it as they passed, but Tristan, in spite of his blindness, seemed to realize that it was there and turned his face toward it.

His parents had died here, I thought. And he had not been able to save them.

It was too dark for them to show me the black sails, so we went home with the woman whose daughter had given me the doll. We ate lentil stew for supper. The woman apologized, saying that they didn't have anything better, because all the farm animals had been eaten by Gurmun long before.

I told her the stew was the most delicious thing I had ever had, and I wasn't exaggerating. Maybe it tasted better because I was so tired, or because there was magic all around us.

The woman set up an old pull-out couch for us, and my dreams were strange that night—about me doing lots of heroic things with my magical powers—but when I woke up, I didn't know if any of them were possible. I'd find out, I guessed, once we got home and I had a chance to think of something besides bare survival.

The dream made me understand better why people would want to live in Curvenal, though. With all this magic around, the air felt lighter, brighter, and, well, more magical. Like there were more possibilities in life. I didn't know how it would be for people who didn't have magic. They might not feel any difference at all. But for people who did, like me and Tristan, Curvenal would call to them now that Gurmun was gone. I was sure of that.

In the morning, Tristan came out with me and limped toward a cliff that looked over the water. I could see a lot of magical creatures out there now: mermaids in the water, just peeking their heads out, and centaurs on the shore. There were fairies with gossamer wings and what looked like trolls. Those were the ones I recognized from my old dream of Gurmun devouring magic.

But there were also creatures I didn't remember, ones that I thought were one thing when I looked from one angle, but then they moved and seemed like something else. Goats that were also snakes, giant butterflies that could blink in and out of existence (or just my vision), what looked like a baby dragon about four feet tall, and the black sails.

There was a whole flock of them, in the air above the water. Huge birds with delicate, billowing wings, they looked like black ship sails while they were in flight.

Tristan must have sensed they were there, because he put his fingers to his lips and whistled to one.

It floated down beside him and spread its wings on the ground, stretching out some hundred feet. I was cautious, wondering if these things were really tame.

"This is how I got to Tintagel," he said. "Now you can return." He waved and seemed pretty cold toward me.

"Wait a minute. You're sending me back without you?" What had happened? I thought we were in love and all that. True love, burning forever, nothing could stop it, not even Gurmun.

"I can be of no use to you now," said Tristan. "I will live out my days here, and my people will pity me, but honor me for my sacrifice."

"You mean because you're blind?"

He would not answer, but he pressed his lips so hard they went white.

"No way. You are coming with me. My mom can heal you, and you have to finish high school, anyway." What chance did he have of getting a good job if he didn't even have a high-school diploma? And he needed a good job, because the whole magic thing didn't seem like it was going to pay very well for either of us.

"But what if she cannot heal me?" he asked.

"Then we'll both learn to live with it. Love conquers all, didn't you know that?" I tugged on his arm and guided him to the waiting black sail. There was just enough room for the two of us on its back.

"I do not want your pity," said Tristan.

"I don't pity you. I pity anyone who has to deal with you if you ever get sick again. Talk about a bad patient," I said, teasing him.

Tristan hesitated for a moment, then gave me his big smile again. How I loved that smile. "I love this island. I think a part of me will always be at home here."

"Maybe we'll come back someday," I said.

"When the pain has healed," said Tristan.

"When my mom has—" I started, but then realized that wasn't the kind of pain he meant. He meant the pain of having his parents die for him.

I guess I understood that pretty well. My dad had died for me. It wasn't something you got over easily. I thought I could handle it now, most of the time. But for me, it wasn't as fresh.

"There are things for us to do in the regular world," I said. "Important things." Like opening the non-magical world back to magic, if Mom said it was okay now that Gurmun was dead. It would have to be done carefully, and only to those who were trustworthy enough not to misuse magic.

Whether the world was ready for magic was another question. Maybe Mom and I would have to talk about that later.

Chapter 28

Together, Tristan and I rode on the black sail toward the rising sun. It was less scary than the ride in the skiff, because we didn't go as fast, and I could relax with the rhythm of the sail's beating wings.

It was still morning when we circled over Tintagel, and the black sail landed a few blocks away from my house, in an open field.

I helped Tristan off and guided him home. Outside the house, there was a faint smell of magic still in the air, but the bodies of all the animals Gurmun had sent against us had disappeared. I didn't know if that was because the animals had never been real—just magical—or because Mom and Mark had taken care of disposing them.

I opened the door and called for Mom. She came running, along with Mark, and together we got Tristan to the couch.

"Izzie, what happened?" asked Mark. "Are you okay?"

"I'm fine, but Tristan's blind. Serpent poison," I said, more for Mom's sake than for Mark's.

When we'd left the house two nights ago, Branna had been lying on the couch, still injured, but she walked into the room a few minutes later. She seemed mostly recovered from the giant's attack. In fact, she looked better than ever. There was a glow about her that I had never seen before. I didn't think I'd ever had that glow with Mark—but I had it now. Even with Tristan's being blind, he was mine and I was his, and that made all the difference in the world.

"Izzie, I need your help," said Mom. She had a vial in her hand. "Keep him calm," she added, because Tristan was turning his head to the side, refusing the potion.

I sat down next to him and rubbed his arm. "Tristan, it's okay. It's Mom's potion. It will help you feel better." He immediately went still.

"If you need any more help, I can sit on him," Mark offered. I waved him off.

Mom poured the potion gently into Tristan's mouth. He made a face, but he swallowed it.

She went into the kitchen and brought back another potion, which she made him drink, too. Later that night, she brought a third.

"Is it that bad?" I asked, not wanting to hear her tell me that he wouldn't see again.

Mom smiled. "That one is to make sure he keeps his hair when he gets older. Just a little thing from me to you."

"Isolde," said Tristan after a long moment. His hands were over his eyes.

I moved to his side eagerly. "Yes? Do you need something?"

He looked into my eyes, and I could tell that he saw me, that his sight had come back. "No, not anymore. I think I will never need anything else, for the rest of my life, but the sight of your beautiful, loving face." I had never been so happy before.

Mom pushed me out of the way so she could check him. "He looks fine," she said at last.

"So that means he won't have any problems with his sight, ever again?" I asked.

"Well, I can't guarantee he won't lose sight when he gets older, but it will be the same as any other age-related sight loss, I think."

"Will you let me stick around with you long enough to see you need glasses for old age?" I asked Tristan.

Tristan answered me with a kiss so long and passionate that Mom had to walk away.

"You know, I would have loved you even if you had been blind forever," I told Tristan.

"And I would have loved you if you had not come back and killed Gurmun," said Tristan. "But luckily, we don't have to."

"Luckily," I agreed.

Later, Mom came back in to remind me I should let Tristan rest.

"Tristan is still weak," said Mom. "And he needs time to recover." She told Tristan he could stay with us, since he didn't have anywhere else to go. Or, she said, he could go to the hospital again.

Needless to say, he did not choose to go to the hospital. Instead, he slept on our couch, and Mark slept on the living-room floor in a sleeping bag. Branna shared the bed in my room. I guess Branna and Mark could have gone home, but they'd been waiting for us, and now they wanted to hang out and make sure things were okay with Tristan.

The next morning, Branna asked, "What is this?" She was holding out the crocheted doll from the girl in Curvenal.

"A gift," I said.

Branna sniffed it. "Who is it from?" she asked suspiciously.

"Someone who had nothing else to give."

Branna looked as if she wanted to ask more, but she didn't. She handed the doll back to me, and I put it on the shelf above my bed.

Two days after we got back, Branna's parents called and demanded to see her. Mark finally took her home. She didn't really need Mom's potions anymore.

When they were gone and Tristan was asleep, Mom and I sat in the kitchen and argued about magic and whether we should come out in public about the truth. I wanted to tell people, to protect them from Mel Melot and others like him. Mom said we would be deluged with reporters and people who wanted love potions that worked better than the one I had tried on the Internet.

"I don't want to tell reporters about it. At least, not yet."

"Well, I've always said you could tell people that you know well," said Mom. "As long as they agree to keep it secret."

"I know, Mom. It's not a matter of calling the newspapers. Just telling more and more people. Not one or two."

I was thinking about Mark's whole posse, for example, and a few others at school.

It was only a start, but after I explained about Mel, Mom nodded. "You know, Izzie, I think your father would be proud of you."

"Does this mean you agree with me about the magic?"

"Yes."

Later Tristan and I talked about it, too. "The people of Curvenal should be allowed to come out and live in the rest of the world. And other people should be able to go there and visit," I said.

Tristan thought about it. "I wouldn't want the beauties of Curvenal to become cheapened," he said. "All the magic there should be honored, not sold off to the highest bidder."

I could see what he meant. "But Branna and Mark could go there sometime. We could show them the black sails." They were my best friends, both of them, and I wanted them to be able to see what I had seen.

Mark and Branna came back over a couple of nights later, and I was surprised at how easy they were with each other. It was like they had been together for a year already, the way Branna seemed to anticipate what Mark was going to say, and how he moved to match her.

I couldn't believe I hadn't seen how right they were for each other. There is more than one kind of blindness, but I had recovered from mine without the help of potions.

Mark and Branna sat on the couch, his hand on her leg, her arm wrapped around his waist. The jealousy, the competition, the anger were gone. We all had what we wanted, and we could just talk about what would happen next.

"We can't go back to school, obviously," said Mark. "The school district has offered to bus us to Parmenie for the rest of the year." He made a face. "Or we can do some online high-school classes and take work-study credits if we help with the cleanup and the rebuilding."

"How long do you think it will take?" I asked.

Mark shook his head. "Six or seven months at least. We have to do the cleanup before we can really figure out how bad the damage is to the foundation. And the district wants to make sure any new building is up to modern earthquake codes, in case anything like this ever happens again."

"It won't," I said.

Mark looked at me. "Are you sure?"

"I'm sure," I said.

"No more magical creatures attacking you?" asked Branna. "How can you be sure of that?"

"Well, I don't think so," I said. "Not this year, anyway."

Mom came in with a tray of drinks.

"Um, I hope you don't take this the wrong way," said Branna, "but at this point I don't think I want to drink anything I haven't seen come out of a hermetically sealed container. Not unless I'm dying and have no other choice."

"It's not a potion," said Mom.

"Or a love philtre," I added. "Not that you need one, you two."

"It's just lemonade," said Mom. "And you can give me a truth serum for that, if you don't believe me."

· · ·

The next week, Tristan and I met Mark and Branna at the school. One of the teachers was there with a crew of kids, all of them wearing hard hats and orange vests. He didn't let them use any of the heavy equipment, but they searched through rubble in the parking lot and made notes.

Tristan was really interested, but I didn't think it was for me. I felt a little adrift until Mom came up behind me.

"Oh, you surprised me. I thought you would be at work," I said.

"I quit," said Mom.

My eyes went wide. "What? But that's what you've always done. Helping people with magic."

"It was one way to help people. The best way I could think of at the time, when I was trying to keep you safe and not show my magic openly. But I think you're right. It's time for a change."

"So what are you going to do?"

"Actually, I was hoping you would do it with me," said Mom. "Along with some online classes so you graduate from high school on time, that is."

"I'm not a witch like you," I said. "What use would you have for me?"

"I'm going to look for people who have latent magic. At the high school, around town, maybe elsewhere."

"Latent magic?" I echoed.

"Well, when we lived in Curvenal, everyone knew what magic they had from birth. But there has been magic in the world for a long time, and many people tried to conceal their magic. It's possible there are thousands of people who have powerful magic just waiting to be revealed. And it could be dangerous if it comes out without them knowing what it is or how to control it."

"That makes sense," I said.

"I'm going to start with Branna," said Mom. She nodded in her direction. "I thought I should tell you."

"You think Branna has magic?" I asked.

"I wonder. She believed in it so easily when you told her. And the fact that she was drawn to you in the first place may mean something. And there's that great-aunt with visions, the one she was named after."

"The rich one," I said thoughtfully. You could use magic to get rich if you wanted to.

"So do you want to help?"

"I think so," I said. I was glad Mom would have something else to do besides watch over me all the time. I was tired of that. And Tristan had taken over that job quite nicely now.

I watched as Mom went over and tapped Branna on the shoulder. I didn't hear what she said, but I saw Branna nod slightly, then nod again. She looked over at me.

I gave her a thumbs-up sign.

That night, Mark and Tristan came back to our house, looking tired but happy, dust all over them. Mark was repeating some joke I didn't get, so I guessed they were friends again.

"What about Mel Melot?" I asked. "Anyone heard from him?"

"Actually, I heard he left town the day after the earth-quake," said Mark.

"Really? Why?"

"Well, the rumors are that he started babbling about magic and giants and potions. His parents were feeling pressure to send him to a therapist, for post-traumatic stress or something like that. Because of the school falling down," said Mark.

"But they didn't?" I have to admit, I felt a certain amount of satisfaction, thinking that Mel Melot had told a little too much of the truth himself in the end. It seemed fair that it got him into trouble.

"He ran away first and took a bunch of family heirlooms with him. His parents swore out an arrest warrant against him because they were so valuable."

"Hmm," I said. I guess his family really was scary.

After dinner, Branna and Mark went home, and Mom left me and Tristan alone in the kitchen to do the dishes.

"I am going to go look for my own apartment," he said.

"Not going to just live under bridges and overpasses, then?" I said, though I was really going to miss having him so close by all the time. I could see that it mattered to him, though. He had come from Curvenal, and that would always make him a little different from other boys my age.

"This time I know I'm staying," he said quietly.

I took his hand and pulled him out to the porch, and we watched the sunset. We stared into the dark sky as the stars began to appear.

"Are you thinking of home?" I asked Tristan.

"You are my home now, Isolde," he said. "Wherever you go, I will follow."

"Except if I ask you not to," I said.

He answered gravely, "Except then."

I laughed. "Good thing you don't have to worry about that."

He kissed me, and it was a kiss of safety and happiness, and there was plenty of heat in it, too. Magical and non-magical.

Epilogue—Two Years Later

Tristan and I were standing on the rocks above the shore of Curvenal, Mark and Branna just behind us.

"Is this it?" asked Branna.

"This is it," I said. Curvenal looked completely different from the way it had been the first time I was here. The ash was gone. Ruined buildings had been torn down and new ones put up in their places.

Most important of all, the cage where Tristan's parents had been held was gone. In its place was a new school.

We heard children laughing behind us. They ran up and down the new playground that Tristan and Mark had built after fixing up Tintagel High. Tristan and Mark had learned a lot. Mark was planning to work construction here in Curvenal. Branna had graduated early and was working on her teaching degree. She was going to do her student teaching in Curvenal, adding to the regular curriculum what she had learned from my mother about magic.

"I guess I don't really wish I had been here then. By all reports it was pretty awful," said Branna.

"Yes," said Tristan tightly. This was only the second time he had come back, and it was still hard on him to be here.

Mom was still out in the non-magical world. She had sold the house in Tintagel and was going around the country pretending to be a motivational speaker. Really, she was just looking for people who had magic.

"I hope you never have to experience something like that, Branna," I said. The battle with Gurmun had made me realize how much I loved Tristan, but it wasn't something I thought of fondly.

"Well, there was that little dragon that we had to deal with a couple of days ago," said Mark.

"What?" asked Branna.

Mark shrugged. "It was going around torching things. Too little to be mean, but we had to do something."

I put my hand on Tristan's shoulder. He was so tense it was like touching a statue of him. "Come on," I said. "No point in brooding."

"I guess not," he said. But he was quiet as we walked back to the school.

"So, are you excited about going to Germany?" asked Branna.

"Yeah. I'm excited about all the old magic we'll learn about." Branna's great-aunt had turned out to be a witch, like Mom, and she had invited me and Tristan to come live with her while we went to the University of Heidelberg, which now was open about being one of the premier magical universities in the world. "The Rhine river maidens and the treasure, for a start. Maybe we'll be able to find it."

"You're not afraid that will be more trouble than it's worth?" asked Branna.

It was a good question. But before I could answer it, I suddenly saw a plume of fire rising in the distance, and my heart almost leaped out of my chest.

"Gurmun," I whispered. Could it be?

Tristan put his hand behind his back and slipped out Excoriator.

We looked up into the sky but didn't see anything.

"Ahem," said Mark, directing our attention downward to another baby dragon, not more than two feet high. He went over and picked it up by the tail, swung it around, and knocked it unconscious, then used steel wire to wrap its mouth shut. He looked pretty competent at this by now.

He brought it up to Tristan. "Looks even younger than the last one," he said.

Tristan nodded. "There is an adult dragon somewhere nearby who is hatching eggs," he said.

"Hmm. I guess that will be my new project for the year."

"I could stay and help," offered Tristan.

I grabbed his arm and pulled him away. "No, you could not. I am sure there are plenty of dragons—or other magical and dangerous creatures—for you to fight at Heidelberg."

Tristan grumbled, but then he asked, "So, are you going to marry me yet?" I felt his breath against my ear. He had asked me before, but I had kept him waiting for the right moment.

"Yes," I said.

He went very still for a long moment. "Are you serious?"

"I'm serious," I said.

Mark and Branna must have been watching us, because they came over right away. "Make her happy," Mark said. "Or you know I'll make you regret it."

Branna gave Mark a loving look. "We're thinking of getting married soon, too," she said.

I smiled. "I think you'll be very happy."

"We will," said Branna. "When you're with the right person, it doesn't matter what else happens. Dragons, giants, slurgs, and serpents. You can still be happy through it."

"I'm going to miss you, Branna," I said.

"I know," she said. "I'll miss you, too. But you've got important things to do. And so do I."

Later that night, Tristan held up Excoriator with one arm, his other firmly around my waist. We flew up and over Curvenal in a long circle and then headed east, over the big cities and out to the Atlantic Ocean. My magic gave us light, and his gave us speed.

Author's Note

I was drawn to do a retelling of the Tristan myth because of the magical elements of the story, which make it stand out from other epic love triangles. I was fascinated by the magical love philtre made by powerful witch women, the giant to be slain, the serpent/dragon with the poisonous bite, and the magical tests of virtue given to Isolde. Tristan was also one of the first epics I read while studying German literature in college. Written by Gottfried von Strassburg in 1211, it is in many ways the first truly German piece of literature that has survived, along with a handful of other tales (including the Nibelungenlied and Parzival) written in the emerging colloquial language rather than Latin. When Richard Wagner was looking for German stories to retell, *Tristan and Isolde* was one that he used for his opera of that name in 1865.

Gottfried's epic begins with a prequel, the love story of Tristan's parents, Rivalin and Blanchefleur. Their lives end tragically (but romantically), and then Tristan grows up in Cornwall and comes to his uncle King Mark's court in Tintagel. Tristan is a musician and a trickster, and he is good at just about everything he tries. He is first introduced to the court by his skill at cutting up a deer ("excoriating" it). I have tipped my hat to this scene in the original with the name of Tristan's sword.

After proving himself in battle several times, Tristan goes to Ireland to deal with Duke Gurmun, who is demanding tribute of King Mark. Tristan proves himself a hero by slaying Gurmun's monstrous brother Morold in single combat, and then finds himself battling a dragon-like serpent. He is nearly killed, but is found and saved by Isolde and her mother, Queen Isolde, both practitioners of herbal magic. He calls himself "Tantris" as a ploy to disguise his true identity, and when Isolde discovers the truth she is ready to kill him—literally—in his bath. But her mother and Tristan persuade her that it is time to forge an alliance with King Mark, and she eventually agrees to a betrothal. Queen Isolde sends a love potion to make young Isolde and King Mark happy in marriage, but on the ocean crossing, Tristan and Isolde accidentally drink it instead and fall helplessly and irrevocably in love.

Nonetheless, Isolde marries King Mark, as is her duty. I have added the idea in my retelling that Brangane loves Mark herself. But in the original, Brangane is Isolde's loyal companion throughout the epic and frequently helps Isolde and Tristan escape discovery from the king and others who are searching for ways to prove them false. One of the most memorable scenes is when the dwarf Melot catches the two lovers and demands that they be tried in court. In another case, Isolde is forced to hold a hot iron. If she lies, she will be burned, but she says the truth so cleverly that she does not give herself away. I have twisted this into Mel Melot, who has a truth potion he forces Isolde to drink.

Gottfried's romance is unfinished, but in most variants, Tristan marries Isolde of the White Hands, who appears later in the story, though he remains in love with the first Isolde. When Tristan has been wounded and can only be cured by Isolde's magical herbs, the jealous Isolde of the White Hands fatefully tells him that she sees a black sail instead of a white one, which means that Isolde has not come for him. Tristan dies in despair, and then Isolde dies of grief when she finds him. I tried to make a happier ending in my version, as tastes in romance have changed with time.

Still, I think the idea of this retelling is very much in the spirit of a medieval tale. Bards in that time borrowed freely from one another, and copying was seen as a kind of tribute. The way a storyteller became well known was to tell an old story to a new audience, adding details that would make sense to the new court and the storyteller's patron. So, changing the ending and resetting this story in an American high school seems to me to be exactly what would make sense to Gottfried. I imagined him cheering me on as I reused, reinvented, twisted, and added to his original.